Praise for

HOW IT WENT DOWN

"Kekla Magoon deftly renders us witnesses to an all-too-common news flash in uncommon, unflinching prose. Gripping to the end."
—Rita Williams-Garcia, Newbery Honor recipient, National Book Award finalist, and Coretta Scott King Award winner

"Thoughtful and compassionate, beautifully composed, this book takes us inside what we think we know and shows us more."
—Helen Frost, Printz Honor recipient

"A hard-hitting look at the ripple effects of one act of violence on an entire community. *How It Went Down* is engrossing and real—it's the right book at the right time."
—Coe Booth, *Los Angeles Times* Book Prize winner

"Through Magoon's deft storytelling—reminiscent of classics in the genre, from Alice Childress' *A Hero Ain't Nothin' But a Sandwich* to the essential *Shooter* by Walter Dean Myers— we become acquainted with members of Tariq's close-knit family, teens who knew him, and their relatives and neighbors."
—*Los Angeles Times*

"A story torn from today's headlines . . . Magoon's novel
brings us into the thick of this all-too-believable tragedy with
a chorus of narrators."
—*Chicago Tribune*

"The many voices provide poignant insights into the forces
at play in the impoverished neighborhoods, where joining a gang
is tough to resist, but the various perspectives also offer
compelling and plausible insights into the way perceptions and
preconceptions shape narratives and affect our actions."
—*The Bulletin*

"A powerful novel that will resonate with fans of Myers's
Monster and Woodson's *Miracle's Boys*."
—*The Horn Book*

"Heartbreaking and unputdownable."
—*School Library Journal*

"Kekla Magoon's books just keep getting better. . . .
[This is] an important, compelling story that everyone should
read, especially high school students trying to make sense
of our supposed post-racial world."
—*BookPage*, A Teen Top Pick

HOW IT WENT DOWN

KEKLA MAGOON

HENRY HOLT AND COMPANY • NEW YORK

SQUARE
FISH

An imprint of Macmillan Publishing Group, LLC
175 Fifth Avenue
New York, NY 10010
fiercereads.com

Square Fish and the Square Fish logo are trademarks of Macmillan and are
used by Henry Holt and Company, LLC under license from Macmillan.

Our books may be purchased in bulk for promotional, educational, or business
use. Please contact your local bookseller or the Macmillan Corporate and
Premium Sales Department at (800) 221-7945 ext. 5442 or by
e-mail at MacmillanSpecialMarkets@macmillan.com.

Library of Congress Cataloging-in-Publication Data is available

ISBN 978-1-250-06823-1 (paperback)   ISBN 978-1-62779-159-5 (ebook)

Originally published in the United States by Henry Holt and Company
First Square Fish Edition: 2015
Book designed by April Ward
Square Fish logo designed by Filomena Tuosto

7   9   10   8

AR: 8.0 / LEXILE: HL560L

*For my Champagne Sisters, in gratitude
for the perspective they offer*

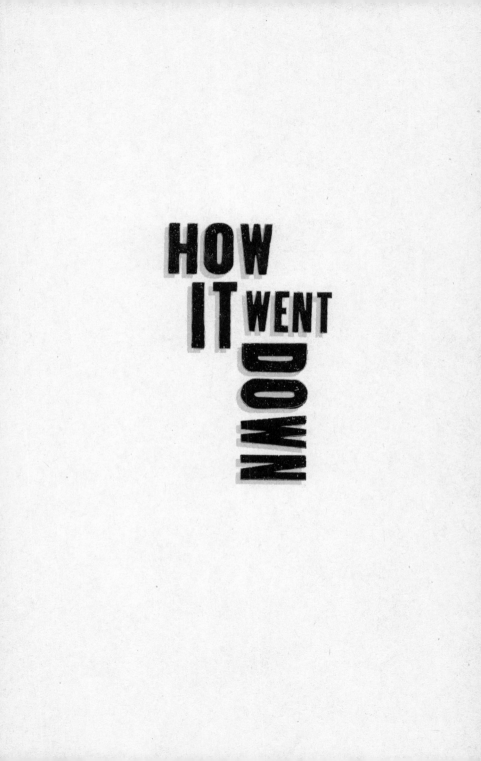

THE INCIDENT

The known facts surrounding the shooting death of sixteen-year-old Tariq Johnson are few. On the evening of June 2, at approximately 5:30 P.M., Johnson sustained two nine-millimeter gunshot wounds to the torso. Police officers arrived at 5:37 P.M. Johnson was pronounced dead at 6:02 P.M. by EMTs at the scene. Police apprehended a person of interest, Jack Franklin, who was present when Johnson was shot but left the scene in a borrowed vehicle shortly afterward. Franklin was pulled over nearly four miles away from the site of the shooting, at 5:56 P.M. A nine-millimeter handgun, recently fired, was found in the back seat.

1. PULSE

JENNICA

Red. Black. White. That's all I remember. It was a blur, like a dream sequence in the sort of movie that comes with subtitles.

Red. Blood, spreading like spilled ink.

Black. His hair and skin, and the tar beneath him. He was kind of sprawled out, and it seemed almost right for him to be down there, like he blended in.

White. I couldn't make sense of it at first. It wasn't clean white, like snow. More of a wispy, dirty white, like clouds on an average winter day. I found out later he had a carton of milk in his hand. It got a bullet right through it, started leaking like a drain and puddling up on the pavement.

The spilled milk seemed wronger than the blood, somehow. I keep thinking that.

BRIAN TRELLIS

I'm not sure I had time to blink. It was over in a minute.

My brain coiled around the knowledge: *The boy in the hoodie has been shot.* The loud sound echoed in my ears, as did his final whimper. The soft clatter-crash of his fall. The sound—yes, the *sound*—of the look the shooter gave me. It had a voice, that look. Sharp and clear like a bell.

I ended up kneeling beside him, the wrecked, bleeding boy. Flat-looking now, so flat.

My hands got dirty. Sidewalk dust, glass shards, blood.

I got blood on my lip. One nervous dart of my tongue, and I tasted it. My throat filled with the need to retch.

Nothing happened.

Except I was blinking now. Blinking down at the boy.

His eyes were open, unblinking.

NOODLE

They do it in the movies. Reach down and close the dead asshole's eyes. But I wasn't about to touch him.

He stared up at me, and it was fucking creepy.

Jennica knelt beside him, in the spreading gray-white pool. "We got to go," I told her, but she could not be moved.

"One-two-three-four-five," she chanted, though the life was gone from his body.

She wouldn't leave, wouldn't stop crying. I couldn't get her up. She stayed there, pumping on his chest and whatnot, a fierce kinda goddess in the half-light.

"We got to go," I said again, and she looked up at me, eyes like switchblades, like she'd fight to the death to put it all back, put it right. She was striking hot, perfection. All I could think was, *I'm with that.*

If it was up to me, we woulda bugged out right away like the rest of the Kings, but Jennica's too *good* for that.

Every fucking minute, another thing reminds me I'm not good enough for her.

SAMMY

Run. All that was in my mind was *fucking run.*

Couldn't think about T falling, or the guy who shot him getting away. Especially not him getting away.

Couldn't think about T dying, or how easy I coulda stopped it. Especially not how easy.

Maybe he won't die. I tried to think it like a prayer.

T's not a screwup like me. He's lucky. Two shots to the chest—yeah, he could make it. It felt wrong to run, knowing that, but I couldn't stop the steam under my feet.

I kept my eye on Brick's jacket and ran where he led me.

Tried to forget I had a piece in my hand. Sleek metal body, cold and strong.

Clutched in my warm, weak fingers.

I fumbled it down into my belt. Tried to forget I could have helped out Tariq with it, taken his killer down.

The piece felt heavy at my waist. Made running kind of awkward, but I kept on after Brick.

I need a gun. I know that. But what good will it ever do me if, when the moment comes, I can't stand up?

TINA

Siren song
Out the open window
Siren song
Weee-ooo-weee-ooo
Siren song
And I squeeze my eyes shut
Siren song
Fingers in my ears
Siren song
Make it stop
Make it stop now
Sirens mean bad news

2. WHAT THEY SAW

9-1-1 EMERGENCY RESPONSE—CALL LOG

[June 2, 5:32 P.M.–5:36 P.M.]

OPERATOR: 9-1-1, what's your emergency?

CALLER: I need the police. A boy's been shot.

OPERATOR: What's your location, sir?

CALLER: Shot. Some guy just shot the kid in the back. White guy. He pulled over his car and just—like—

OPERATOR: Sir, I'm notifying the police and EMTs. I need an address. Where are you calling from?

CALLER: I'm on Peach Street. They're right outside. 219 South Peach. He's been shot. He's on the ground—

[loud bursting sound, over static]

CALLER: Oh, God. He shot him again.

OPERATOR: Sir?

CALLER: [indecipherable muttering]

OPERATOR: Sir? Can you repeat that? Are you in danger? Please move to a safe location.

CALLER: He's driving away! He's driving away. He's back in his car—

OPERATOR: Sir, the police are on their way.

CALLER: I can see the license. I'm going to try—

[sound of door chimes]

OPERATOR: Sir, please step back inside. Is the shooter still on the scene?

CALLER: Oh, God.

OPERATOR: Sir?

CALLER: There's blood everywhere. [shouts] CPR! We need CPR!

OPERATOR: Is the shooter still on the scene? Sir, please go back inside. The police are on their way.

CALLER: It's a dark blue car. Small. KL7— I can't see. He's just going . . .

OPERATOR: Which direction is he going?

CALLER: Uh . . . straight down Peach. No, he just turned right on Wilson. Or maybe Van Buren. It's a ways down. I could get my car—

OPERATOR: No, sir. Please stay on the scene.

CALLER: [shouts] That's the guy, that's the guy. Blue car, just turned. That's the shooter.

OPERATOR: Sir? Has the shooter returned to the scene?

CALLER: [shouts] Go get him! Go get him!

OPERATOR: Sir, who are you talking to?

CALLER: He can't just shoot and run like that.

OPERATOR: Do not attempt to pursue the suspect. I've relayed the information to the police. They will take care of it. How many people have been shot?

CALLER: One, just one. Oh, God. It's Tariq.

OPERATOR: Tariq?

CALLER: Oh, God. His mama. [shouts] Push harder, girl! You got to blow into his mouth.

[sirens in the background]

OPERATOR: Sir, the police and ambulance will be arriving very shortly.

CALLER: They're coming. They're coming. I've got to go.

OPERATOR: Sir, please stay on the line.

CALLER: I've got to go.

[dial tone]

BRIAN TRELLIS

I was coming out of the hardware store when I heard a guy down the street shouting, "Stop, thief!"

I look, and this is what I see: Farther down the sidewalk, a shop clerk with an apron on comes running out of the convenience store, waving his arms in the air. "Come back here!"

Streaking past me, just right there in front of me, goes a dark face in a black hoodie. The hood's fallen back somewhat, like he can't hold it in place while he's hurrying. He's trotting down the street pretty quick, his shoulders all hunched around his haul. I can see it on his face. He thinks he's home free. He slides past me.

Not so fast, sucker.

I step up after the little fool. There's a bunch of other guys around, but no one's making a move to stop him. By the looks, they're all members of the 8-5 Kings. They don't care enough to stop him, but he's not getting away.

Not on my watch.

I step up, clamp my hand down on his shoulder. I got a big hand, real meaty. Takes all of his shoulder under it like a handlebar. "Not so fast," I tell him. The Kings scare me, sure, but not this little scrap of a kid.

"Hey. Get up off me, yo." He starts squirming. But it's no work at all to hold him. "Come on," he says. "Let me go."

"This is a matter for the police," I say, holding firm.

"What's your problem, man?" he says.

"*Woooooo,*" go the Kings, crowding around us. "Tariq's gonna take down the big man."

I read it all wrong. He wasn't just passing by the Kings; I guess he's one of them. They're calling out to him, egging him on. Maybe it's some kind of initiation.

Hoodie boy struggles. From under his arm, something small, roundish, and firm pushes out at me.

"He's got a gun," I hear someone say. "Shit, back it up!"

I can hold my own in a fistfight, but I'm not about to get shot to save some corner store fifty bucks in loot, or whatever this thug pilfered. I let him go. "Don't shoot." I back away. "I didn't mean nothing by it."

Kid spins around, face all stormy. His arms are full. My heart's pounding. My eyes drop to the gun in his hand. He's facing me now. I'm bracing myself, thinking, *Why'd I have to try and get tough?* Thinking, *I'm about to die.* But it's not right. I'm looking at his hand. Looking for that deadly glint of metal, but there isn't anything, and then out of nowhere, the kid is falling. He buckles like a hinge and drops. I hear a loud noise and the sound of glass breaking. Something liquid splashes over my feet. I jump back, but the kid is just down.

"Oh, shit," someone shouts. "Was that for real?"

"Tariq," someone says.

"We gotta get the fuck out." Someone else.

Three different voices.

I hear another sound, unfamiliar and close. A popping, kind

of pinging, very loud. By the time I turn, what I see is a white man, hustling away. I see people running, ducking. Hear the jingle of bells on a door.

"What happened?" I say it out loud, to the air. "What just happened?"

JENNICA

We were a little high, me and Noodle both. I regret that now, but I can't undo it. We were across the street. I didn't see the first shot, 'cause we were cozying up on the stoop there like normal, but I saw the second one. Tariq was already on the ground. The guy standing over him put a bullet in him, right there on the sidewalk. Then he jumped in his car and drove off.

Noodle said I was like some kind of hero. The guy drove off, and people were screaming, but Noodle said I just walked right across the street to where Tariq was lying. I don't remember doing that.

I do remember I got blood on my hands. From the CPR. I got it on my clothes, too, on everything. I remember being on my knees in this terrible pool and pushing up and down on his chest with my arms locked, like I learned.

We took this class in school last year, about how to save a person's life. I guess I should have signed up for it again this year. I didn't know enough. I couldn't save him.

My eyes got all blurry, and his mouth was all bloody, and I couldn't bring myself to breathe into it. Maybe that was wrong, but I also remember worrying I might blow blood down his throat. Can that happen? I wanted to ask the ambulance man who took over after me, but I couldn't manage the words. I still haven't tried to find out.

I'm not sure I really want to know.

NOODLE

Leave it to Tariq to mess up my afternoon. We were sitting on the stoop, Jennica whispering all sexy in my ear. We were waiting for Brick, but I was about ready to bail on meeting up with the guys and find a quiet place, just the two of us.

Then I heard Tariq's voice, chirping from all the way across the street. Loudmouthed little punk. I quit kissing on my girl and looked over there. Tariq was talking to Brick, who must've come up right about the same time, a couple other guys along with him.

Jennica leaned into my neck, all high and turned on. And I was pissed then, because I should have been enjoying it. But there went T, arms full of milk and stuff. It figured—he would be too cheap to pay Rocky five cents for a grocery sack.

He had some nerve, talking shit to Brick after everything that went down last week.

Brick was trying to get T to step up into the Kings for real, instead of dancing around the edges like he had been. I never could figure why he wanted that chickenshit dabbler as his lieutenant. Neither of them seemed to understand what they were saying when they talked about being number one and number two—that it would make me number three. Plus, Tariq is almost five years younger than me. What, I'm supposed to take a back seat to some punk kid who didn't even really want in? No way should T step up to outrank me. But Brick was determined about it; I still don't get why.

Across the street, Tariq had to go and drag the big, light guy into it. Guy looked like a refrigerator, but T was talking smack, as usual. Now things were looking up, I thought. I'd seen Tariq in a fistfight. He didn't have the skills to go up against a guy that size. Fool. I don't know what Brick saw in that pile of mess.

The Kings crowded in closer to watch the fight. I craned my neck up, trying to see past their shoulders. If Tariq was about to get his ass beat, I was sure as shit gonna be watching. But my view was blocked, partly by the guys and mostly by the car that stopped in the middle of the street.

White dude jumped out. Hauled ass up onto the curb.

Someone—Sammy, I think—shouted, "He has a gun!"

I leaped up, startling Jennica. The Kings backed out, in a loose circle around Tariq and the big man. The big man threw his hands up.

Tariq turned around, facing the new guy. His voice, typically loud. Annoying. "Mind your own business, cracker." All his shit falls out of his hands. One arm stretched out in front.

Then the shots. One, two.

I thought, *Damn. That motherfucker's about to get made.* T's talking shit one minute, the next he smokes a whitey right in front of Brick? That'd earn him a straight shot to the number two spot. No question.

But it was Tariq who fell. Slow motion. The Kings peeled off and scattered. White dude scrambled to his car. The gun in his hand was silver. Nine millimeter. His arm, straight down. Finger still on the trigger. Wild eyes.

I threw myself down on top of Jennica. We landed awkwardly

against the stairs. Her fingers fluttered against my shirt, around my ribs. "Oh, God," she murmured. "Oh, my God."

I stayed like that—I didn't know what else that crazy white bastard might do—until the car rumbled off down the street with a squeal of tires.

"Was that for real?" Sammy screamed.

"We gotta get the fuck outta here," ordered Brick. "Now."

Jennica pushed me off and ran across the street. "Tariq," she cried. She planted her hands on his chest and started CPR. Jake came running out of his liquor store, phone up against his ear, shouting, too. Halfway down the block, another white guy stood frozen, watching.

Jake's voice and Jennica's crying—those were the only sounds on the block. The other Kings had disappeared. Everyone else had gone inside. The rumble of the car faded, became part of the distant background hum.

I followed Jennica across the street. Couldn't see no choice about it—that's my girl. Stood on the curb, looked down at T's flat, leaking body.

He was asking for it, I told myself.

If that guy didn't pop him, someone else was gonna, that's for damn sure. Kid couldn't keep his mouth shut for a hot second, 'less he was stuffing a snack in his face.

Brick must have been tripping; no way was T ever gonna be good enough to replace me. I looked upon his slack cheeks, open eyes, and all I felt was relieved. *Good riddance, Tariq Johnson.*

I was there. I saw the whole thing. Fucker had it coming.

BRICK

You can't fault a brother for getting heated. Tariq be talking shit to me, like usual, coming down the street. That little punk. I taught him everything he knows, then he up and flaked out on me, talking about college and turning his back on his homies.

I shepherded that son. From the time he was little, I saw he had this energy, this flow. He coulda run this street with me, if he put his mind to it. But no.

So, yeah. When he come down the street, talking shit, hell, yeah. I started hassling him back. He was saying shit about my moms. I don't let nobody say shit about my moms. So I start talking about his moms. I see the carton of milk in his hand, and I say something about how he shouldn't have to go to the store so often, 'cause he got a cow at home.

That's when he starts kicking at me. I dodge him easy and start laughing, sure he's gonna blow a whole gasket and start losing all the shit he just bought all over the sidewalk so he can come and get me.

I was howling. Tariq be dancing all over, trying to kick me. He goes, "I'ma come back. I'ma come back in five minutes and I'ma lay you out."

I just go, "*Woooooo.*" All the guys howl behind me, like backup singers.

Some big-ass punk, a pale-looking brother, steps out of a store and grabs Tariq, outta nowhere. We all thought he must have some real bad bone to pick, thought Tariq's ass was about to get whupped into tomorrow, so we crowded around to watch. We was still howling. Tariq and he start tussling.

"Shit, he's got a gun," Sammy says. He's looking over my shoulder, toward the street.

I don't know when Tariq pulled the gun. Next thing I know, big guy's backing off of him, all freaked out. "Don't shoot."

Tariq's still got all the shit in his arms, and he's holding out a gun at the light-skinned punk—blackest motherfucking gun I ever saw.

"Back the fuck off. I'll put a hole in you, cracker," he says.

For a second there, I got real proud of Tariq. I thought, *Fuck college. My boy's coming home to the street.* For a second there, I got real proud.

TOM ARLEN

I had agreed to loan Jack Franklin my car for a few days while his was in the shop. He came down to pick it up round four in the afternoon. We got to talking. The weather was good out there on my back porch, so we cracked a few beers and got to drinking. Couple carefree guys, living the good life. That's what I was thinking.

So I walked Jack outside, showed him the car and all, handed over the keys. We shook hands. He said, "Thanks. You're a lifesaver."

I said, "No problem. Just bring her back to me in one piece."

I watched him pull out of the parallel spot all right. I wasn't too worried about the car—I was just ragging on him for old times' sake. Jack and I go way back. I walked to the corner, waving after him. He didn't get far.

Middle of the next block, he pulled over. I walked that way to catch up, thinking maybe there was a problem with the car.

Then I realized it wasn't the car. There was a whole fracas going on up the block. Bunch of gang members surrounding a white guy. Threatening him, jostling him around in the circle. He towered over all of them, the white guy, but he looked scared shitless. The gang kids called out names at him. Taunting. Chains dangled at their waists, knife sheaths poked out of their baggy pockets. Gave me the shivers.

I stopped at the corner, scared to go any closer. I've never had any problems in the neighborhood from the color of my skin. I keep my head down, go about my business. Most of the people are nice. I steer clear of the gang kids, but so does everyone else.

I didn't like what I was seeing, though. Jack stood up, my car door open. "Hey," he yelled over at the group. "You let him alone."

Jack's a braver man than I am. He walked around the car. I saw him raise up his arm and I thought, *He's gonna go right in there, try to break it up.* I held my breath, thinking they were gonna fold him in, start hassling him.

Instead, they parted. The big white guy stepped backward, out of the circle, holding his hands up like he was under arrest.

Jack moved forward, arm raised. "Let him alone," he said again.

"Mind your own business, cracker," said this scrawny slip of a kid from the center of things. He came forward. His arm was raised too. The gun in his hand . . . Gun!

"Jack!" I called. "Look out!" I didn't know if he could hear me, but I was scared to go any closer.

Pop-pop. The kid staggered forward, fell. The other gang boys scattered. Jack spun in a slow circle. His arm was still raised—he had a gun, too. The big white guy turned toward Jack, looking grateful.

I shook my head. Jack Franklin. Keeping the peace. We were just talking about it, on my porch. About how everything on the streets is going to shit because good citizens are too afraid to stand up.

Look at me, for example. Stuck on the corner, watching it all go down. Unable to do anything about it.

The gang kids started moving back in. Sirens wailed in the background. Jack jumped in the car, drove off. *That's my car*, I thought. *That's my car.* Jack's a braver man than I am, but he drove away in my car.

EDWIN "ROCKY" FRY

Tariq forgot his change, is all. I stepped out in the street to try and catch him. I meant to do the right thing, get the kid his money back. It was a dollar seventy-three.

He'd bought a half gallon of milk, a big pour jar of salsa, two rolls of toilet paper, and a Snickers bar. Paid me with a ten.

I stepped out on the street with the money in my hand. Tried to wave at him. Called out for him to come back. "Tariq!" One of his friends heard me and turned, so I yelled to him, "Hey, stop T, would you?"

I didn't see who started the fighting. They were all gathered around, like they do sometimes, whooping and hollering. I lost sight of Tariq in the middle of it. I went back inside, because I don't want any trouble. I don't want to see anything. Don't want to have to answer questions later.

I put Tariq's change in an envelope. Wrote his name on it. I knew he'd be back in about five minutes. His mother would know exactly how much change she was supposed to get, and she'd send him down after it. I'd keep it for her. I try to be a good neighbor like that. I don't want any trouble.

I heard the shots. I heard the screaming and the shouting and the sound of the car squealing away from the curb.

I didn't know it was Tariq. Not till later. Even if I had known, I wouldn't have gone out there. I don't want any trouble.

His mother never came down for the change. Not surprising, really. It was a dollar seventy-three. One round dollar, two quarters, two dimes, and three pennies. I still got those coins.

SAMMY

Tariq was my friend. I ain't gonna tell nobody what I seen.

I try to figure out how T would want it to be known, but it ain't that easy.

Brick and them got all puffed up and proud, thinking T was armed and ready to waste Jack Franklin. T woulda liked them thinking that.

Except it's not just them who seen it. And no one else was supposed to know how T was coming up in the Kings. T ain't want his momma to find out, or his sister, or even Tyrell. That was his deal with Brick, for the time being. They was fighting about it just the other day.

How you gonna be a King and not sport the colors? What kinda half-ass join is that? I agreed with Brick on that point.

But T was all set on the way he wanted to do it. So he woulda been stupid to have a gun on him, just walking to the grocery store. Real stupid.

T wasn't stupid. That much I'll tell anybody.

We was walking down the sidewalk, heading to meet Noodle, when T come up the other way. He started trading words with Brick, real vicious, but that was to be expected. It was all gonna blow over fine in a minute, until the light dude ran up on us.

T dropped his shit to fight the guy. Dropped everything, except the candy. I knew it was for Tina. Always with them Snickers, that girl. Anytime she could get her hands on one.

I looked away, because I didn't want to see T get his ass beat. I looked out over the street and saw Jack Franklin come running. Had his arm outstretched.

"Shit," I blurted. "He's got a gun!"

The pale brother let go of Tariq and threw up his hands. Jack Franklin kept on coming. Tariq turned around. He put his arms out in front of him. "Back off, cracker," he shouted. "Mind your own damn business."

Jack Franklin shot him in the chest. One shot—*BOOM*—and Tariq folded. His arms flew upward as his body went down, like a creepy winged thing. When I close my eyes, it's all I see.

BOOM. The second shot was just a sound; I must have closed my eyes then, too.

Everyone better stop asking me if T had a gun in his hand. They better stop wondering, if he did, what could've happened to it. All the cops found at the scene, by his body, was that goddamn bar of Snickers.

Franklin only thought he saw a gun.

3. RIPPLE EFFECTS

KIMBERLY

"Oh, good lord," says the woman in my styling chair. "Is it ever going to stop?" She plugs her ears with dainty fingertips, impeding my progress at trimming her ends. I was barely aware of the sirens until she pointed them out.

"Careful of your nails," I remind her. Coi just gave her a manicure.

The woman lowers her hands and looks. As if her nails would ever chip. She's that kind of woman, the impossibly put-together kind. She comes in once a month, like clockwork, for a trim and blowout.

"What do you think happened?" she says, craning her neck. The painted words on the windows make it difficult to really see much out there. I like it that way. The salon is a nice oasis from the city's grit and grime and noise.

But, come to mention, there are kind of a lot of sirens. They go rushing past our windows, swirling and screaming full tilt. Cop cars first, and after a minute, an ambulance. After the sirens fade, the strobe lights still pulse up the block. Whatever happened, it wasn't far away.

There's always something crazy going on, between the cops and the Stingers and the Kings and their corner dope guys, turf wars and so on and so on. All hell breaks loose just often enough to remind everyone how screwed up this neighborhood is. As if we could forget we live in the beating heart of the ghetto.

The woman settles back in the chair and re-smooths the magazine in her lap. "I can't see anything," she says. "Anyway, I should try not to be one of those people."

"What people?"

"You know, the ones who rubberneck at car accidents."

It wasn't a car accident. You get maybe one cop for a car accident. But she's a fancy type of woman, from another part of town. The type who only comes down here to get her hair done, because everyone in the city knows if you want black hair done right, you come to Mollie's Manes. Under the salon cape, she's wearing a business skirt suit with smart, expensive-looking heels. Maybe she can't imagine needing a cop for anything other than a car accident.

"They say it's human nature," she says. "To try to see what happened. Natural curiosity. Everyone does it." She gazes at me in the mirror, slightly guilty, silently asking me to agree.

"Sure, I guess." My fingers lift and fan her locks. The customer is always right. Except she isn't. Some of us look away when bad things happen. Some of us don't want to see.

The ambulance is the first to retreat. It rolls away quietly. No flashing. No siren.

False alarm, maybe.

Either that, or somebody died.

NOODLE

The cops come, and we're the only ones still here. Us and the light-skinned big man, the one who got into it with Tariq.

The paramedics come too, with their scissors and gauze. Ease Jennica out of their way. I lift her against me. Tariq's blood on her gets on me, and that makes it realer. I mean, I don't take it back, what I said about him having it coming. Tariq was a hot mess. But it hurts now, that that's what I been thinking.

The cops come, try to separate us. "We need to take your statements," they say.

"We been together all along," I answer. "We saw it the same." Jennica could have picked any guy, any King. I color myself lucky that she's got her arms around me. I'm not letting her go.

Cops shift and mutter, but that's just how it is. I wonder if they know we're high, if they're looking past it. Jennica leans against me, lays a bloody hand on the skin of my arm. I think, *This was one good, sexy high ruined.*

Jennica tells it how she saw it.

I say, "Nothing to add. The white guy did it."

They ask questions.

"No," she's saying. "Tariq didn't have a gun."

I keep a hold on her, keep my mouth shut. What do I care if the cops get the story straight? I don't know where she was looking, though. Tariq sure as shit had a gun in his hand. Where it's got to by now? Anyone's guess. I wonder, too, why he didn't pull the trigger. He coulda saved himself. He shoulda.

Damn. Maybe I do take it back, at least a little. He had it coming, but it didn't have to come.

Cops hand us paperwork, asking us to sign.

Damn. Tariq shoulda smoked that cracker. Then we coulda bugged out, all together. Woulda spared us all a lot of trouble.

TYRELL

I'm at the dinner table, by the window, doing homework. Math's the easiest, so I saved it for last. After this I can go out and hang. I'm doing calculus problems, differential equations. Plus x, minus two.

TV's on in the background. I like that low sound—makes me feel less alone.

Shooting, I hear the reporters say. *Downtown. Peach Street.*

I look out the window, not at the TV, because I live on Peach. The street looks quiet. Whatever happened must be farther down.

I reach for my cell, at the edge of the place mat. I call Tariq's number, see if I can get the skinny. T always knows what's going down.

Phone just rings and rings.

TINA

Tariq goes, *I'll pick you up some candy. If there's change.*
I go, "Yeah, right."
Tariq goes, *You think I won't?*
I go, "You always say that, and you always forget."
Tariq goes, *Nuh-uh.*
I go, "What you gonna bring me?"
Tariq goes, *I know what you like.*
I go, "Shoot. You gonna forget."
Tariq goes, *Naw. But if you keep talking trash,*
I just might get hungry on the way back.
Bring you home a wrapper.
I go, "Tariq!"
Tariq goes.
I wait.
I wait.
I wait so long, I'm sure he forgot.

VERNESHA

Tina's bouncing off the walls, wondering where's Tariq? I am wondering that myself. I sent him out an hour ago, for an errand that should have taken ten minutes. I don't generally mind it when he stays out with his friends, but he's due back for supper, and I sent him because I needed those things.

Milk for Tina to drink with supper. Salsa for the tacos for the rest of us. We're down to about five squares on the toilet paper roll.

I can count on Tariq. Sure, he's a goof most of the time, but I can count on him.

The food is ready. All the plates laid out.

"Vernie," Mama says to me, "we best just eat 'fore it gets cold."

I don't want to eat. There's a lurching wave in the pit of my stomach. It doesn't go away, especially when someone starts pounding at the door.

REDEEMA

Cops got a special way of knocking at the door. With the meat of the fist. Sets the whole wall a-shaking.

Next thing that comes—it ain't never good news.

MELODY

Peach Street is messy and crowded this evening. I shoulda gone another way. Yellow police tape, flashing sirens. Barricades closing the block between Simpson and Roosevelt. It's just cop cars, no police vans or SWAT-looking guys. It's not a drug bust. Maybe a robbery, or a shooting? Something to avoid, anyway.

I turn off of Peach, take the long way. Better than wading through a sea of law enforcement. I wonder what happened, of course, but it's always better to mind your own business.

Ms. Rosalita sits in her usual lawn chair, in front of the fence at the community garden. It's unusual for her to be all alone; generally there are several elders from the neighborhood sitting in that spot.

"Melody, baby. What's going on over there?"

I take her wrinkled hands in mine. "I don't know, Ms. Rosalita. Something pretty bad."

She closes her eyes, and the folds in her face seem ancient. Her lips move in a silent prayer.

I head on into my building. The elevator door is about to slide shut.

"Hold the elevator," I call, but the door keeps closing. I put on some steam, because if I miss it, I'll be waiting ten minutes. Jam my foot in the crack, with no time to spare.

"You ain't hear me?" I scold, pushing the door back open.

It's Sammy Neff standing in there. He's got on low dark jeans and a long red T-shirt. Arms crossed over his chest, held tight.

"Hey, Sammy." I get in the box with him. Push my floor. And his. Doofus ain't even pushed the button yet.

He stares at the mishmashed elevator floor tiles.

"You okay?" I ask him. To be honest, he looks kinda deep-fried.

He jumps like he's just now seeing me. "Oh. Hey." He drops his arms and puffs up his chest.

I shake my head. Boys. Always fronting.

The door glides closed again. Slowest elevator in the world. We're gonna be in here for a minute.

"Tariq Johnson got shot," he whispers. "They're saying he's dead."

4. COLORS

TYRELL

I wake up annoyed. I sent Tariq about a dozen texts last night, trying to find out what went down on Peach Street. Knowing T, he was right there in the mix of it. Why is he ignoring me? It ticks me off. He probably knows everything, and he's not telling. Sometimes he likes to get dramatic and tell it all in person, but the least he could do is text back.

Except he doesn't. I drag myself into the kitchen and put in some toast. While it crisps, I go in the living room and flip on the news. I have the house to myself this time of the morning. Both my parents go off to work before six, which is when I get up. So I make the toast and slice up an apple and listen with half an ear as the morning-show people chat about something to do with floral arrangements. I wash my hands and shove the apple core down the disposal. When I shut off the water, I hear: . . . *neighborhood known as Underhill. Police have finally released the name of the teen slain there last night . . . and I believe we have a picture? Just a second here . . .*

That's weird. This is a national newscast. Why would they be talking about my neighborhood?

I carry my breakfast into the living room, listening. This'll show T—I don't need to get all my info from him.

REVEREND ALABASTER SLOAN

"Turn on the TV." My assistant's voice rattles through the phone speaker before I even have a chance to say hello. "This might be the one."

I should be used to these wake-up calls by now, but Kelly usually manages to catch me by surprise.

"What time is it?" I croak, rolling toward the nightstand. "I mean, what channel?"

"Yours." She means the twenty-four-hour news channel that frequently invites me for guest appearances. "It's after six. You weren't up yet?"

"Getting there," I lie.

"It's on the early wires," she says. "I got it from Moira, my friend at the *Washington Post*. You remember her?"

"Uh, yeah, Moira. From the thing that one time?" I remember sizable breasts and the need to speak solely on the record.

"Exactly."

"What are we talking about?"

"A shooting. Inner-city teen shot by a white guy. It's gonna blow up later today."

"How so?" Forgive me the morning cynicism, Lord, but black kids get shot all the time, and no one looks twice. I've been shouting about it at the top of my voice for going on twenty-five years now, and they all just cover their ears.

"You can get a jump on this thing," Kelly says. "Not that many people know about it yet."

"You just told me to turn on the TV."

"The full story hasn't broken yet," Kelly says. "Moira thinks this is only the beginning. She's got a friend who works the police beat for the local news out there, and she . . ."

The phone drops away from my ear as I stretch. My wife is frying bacon; the smell wafts up to me. Something's baking too. Fresh muffins? God Almighty. Women are something holy.

". . . gang-related, but it turns out the kid might not even have been armed." Kelly is still speaking. "They released the shooter from custody early this morning, on the grounds that it was self-defense. But it can't be, because he was barely on the scene before the shooting occurred. This story has race bias coming out of its ears."

"Uh-huh." I scroll through the channels.

Whatever Kelly wanted me to see is over. Now it's a toilet paper commercial. Looks like a good lead to me. I shuffle into the bathroom.

WILL (AKA eMZee)

"Underhill's been on the news," says my stepdad. "The national news."

"What?" I rub my face sleepily, sip my orange juice. These late nights out are killing me. Maybe I should start tagging in the afternoon. It just seems so much less . . . gangster.

"A man shot a gang kid downtown last night," Steve says. "Now it turns out he might not have been a gang member at all. The guy claims self-defense, but the kid wasn't even armed, they think now. Big controversy." His eyes remain glued to the set, probably reading the scroll bar. The volume is set real low.

The kitchen TV is mounted on the wall above the fridge. Steve loves TV. He has six of them in his house, in just about every room, including his bathroom. Mom says, *Stop calling it his house. It's our house, too.* We've been here three years. Still doesn't feel like home.

"Peach Street," Steve says. "You know it?"

I wrinkle my nose at him. Everyone from Underhill knows Peach Street. *Steve* should freaking know Peach Street. Mom and I lived right off it, before we moved to his place across town. But I don't think Steve ever came to our apartment. Not one time in the whole year that they dated. He's a total ghettophobe.

"Yeah, I know it." In fact, that explains the police tape fluttering up and down the block between Simpson and Roosevelt. I saw it last night when I was down there tagging, but I can't tell that to Steve. He'd have my ass. So would Mom.

Steve pumps the volume up a notch.

. . . wearing a black hooded sweatshirt and a red bandanna, easily mistaken for a gang member . . .

Mistaken? That's bull. No one walks down Peach Street wearing a red bandanna by accident.

STEVE CONNERS

These damn kids. They never learn. As a black man, you have to keep your head down. You have to keep yourself steady. You have to follow every rule that's ever been written, plus a few that have always remained unspoken.

How hard is that to understand? Like I always tell Will: If you dress like a hood, you will get treated like a hood. If you want to get treated like a man, you have to dress like a man. Simple as that.

It's how this world works.

It stops being about the color of your skin after a while and starts being about how you comport yourself. Inside, too, but mostly out. If you want to wear your pants down around your knees, with some big old chain dragging them down, a do-rag in your pocket, fine. But you have to understand how it looks. You have to know how people are going to react. Those outfits are associated with an undesirable, often dangerous element of society. Everyone knows that.

I wear a three-piece suit to work every day. That's every single day for the last twenty years, from my first internship out of college all the way up through the ranks to vice president of sales. On the weekends, I favor a sport coat. Everything is tailored, nice. I make a point of looking good. Would I be more comfortable in baggy jeans and a basketball jersey? Of course I would. My favorite shirt is the Michael Jordan #23 Bulls jersey I have hanging in the closet. Twenty-some years old, and it's still in good shape. Mint condition, really. I've never worn it out of the house. I'm a professional. How would that look?

TYRELL

I can't even go to school, once I know. The way it works is, T always comes by in the morning around 7:20 because my place is on his way. He rings my buzzer twice in a rhythm, like *zing . . . ZING*, so I know it's him and I come down.

If he's sick or whatever, he'll call, so I know to go on ahead, but usually then I just skip. I don't like to walk to school alone. It's only ten blocks, but eight of them beeline through the heart of Stinger territory. Sometimes those guys try to lay a sales pitch on you, just like the Kings. *Why you walking all alone, homes? Get yourself a yellow jacket; you ain't never gotta be alone.* They crowd around me, flashing signs and breathing close.

I shiver. T hasn't called. It's five after eight, and there's still no sign. My screen is black, and the air is silent.

My books are all loaded up in my backpack, ready to go, and I wait for the buzzer. My mind hums this kind of static, and I just know the buzz is gonna come. *Zing . . . ZING.*

I'll go running down the stairs. Fling open the door. "You asshole," I'll say. "You freaking punk."

Tariq will be standing there, grinning, one fist on the doorjamb and the other on his hip. "Yo, Ty," he'll say. "I had you going for a minute."

EDWIN "ROCKY" FRY

The cops keep coming around. They want to say Tariq robbed me. I can only tell them he didn't.

"But he had a gun with him?" they ask.

"I didn't see one" is my answer. "I mind my own business."

"Did you feel threatened at any time?"

"He paid his bill, all right? Please. I know his family. Tariq wouldn't pull a stunt like that on me." This is the same boy who always picks up a Snickers bar for his little sister. Girl's a little slow, I guess, but Tariq takes good care of her. Says *please* and *thank you* too, not like those gang boys who were out there razzing him. I never see any of them in here buying milk for their mamas. It's always beer, cigarettes, and Slim Jims.

"So you didn't feel threatened?"

"From Tariq? Never once."

They leave, again and again, unsatisfied.

Now the news people are at it too. Calling Tariq an "armed robbery suspect." I don't know where they get these tales. I've never said a thing against him. Not a single thing to make it sound like that rumor could be true. Who knows where they're getting it.

I used to read the paper in the mornings. Used to take in every word. Now I don't know what to believe.

SAMMY

"They caught the fucker, and they just let him go," Brick says, about as heated as I've ever seen him.

"What'd you expect?" Noodle mutters, from the front passenger seat. We're riding in Brick's car. Radio tuned to the local hip-hop station.

The volume is already cranked, but Noodle cranks it higher. It's a brief news segment; they're talking about Tariq.

. . . member of the 8-5 Kings, shot to death in Underhill yesterday. Yo, Kings, rest easy, fellows—for once, we can report it wasn't a turf war. Cops arrested and released the alleged shooter after he lodged a claim of self-defense. That's right, he's back on the street, ladies and gentlemen. Our best advice? Leave your do-rags at home today. . . .

The radio report is confusing—cops say Tariq had on a red bandanna, but T wasn't sporting no colors yesterday. He was in a black hoodie. Everybody's got one of those. His T-shirt wasn't red or nothing, either.

When the heavy, thumping music comes back, Noodle and Brick resume their argument about the gun. "You were across the street," Brick says. "How could you even see?"

"He didn't have no gun," Noodle protests. "Punk like Tariq? Hell, no."

"I was a foot from him," Brick insists. "You calling me a liar?"

"Ask Jennica. She told it to the cops. You know she wouldn't lie."

Brick looks in the rearview. "Sammy, settle it."

Noodle turns to glare at me over his shoulder. I swallow hard. There's no way to win this.

"I'm not sure," I answer. "All I saw was Jack Franklin."

Brick's never offered to pick me up before. I don't have that kinda clout in the organization. But since I was there last night and the shooting's all he wants to talk about, he rolled by for me. I don't want anything good to come from T dying. But I can't turn my back on this kinda opportunity.

REDEEMA

"You start running with a gang, I'll kill you with my own hands," I said. Them's the last words I ever spoke on his little brown ears. He had that do-rag in his back pocket. Red, with them gourd shapes spread across it in black.

I said it like a joke, though, and he knew it too, 'cause he was smiling. Waved his buns at me like he hot stuff.

"Woo," I said. "Boy, you quit dancing and get back to dusting."

So I s'pose them's the last words, really.

His momma called him up from the kitchen right then. Tariq flashed them little white teeth at me, then go off on her bidding.

Lord, I ain't wanna think about it no more.

That boy be smart. How he gonna leave the house with that do-rag still on him?

Shoulda thrown them all away, come the moment. But we ain't wanna put good cloth to waste. When it got real severe with the colors and the gangs around the neighborhood, we put all them things straight in the rag bin. Gathered 'em all right up, never to leave the house again. I been around a long time. I know how it goes.

I's the one what set him to dusting. A boy's gotta learn to do the small things round the house. I ain't know Vernie was gonna up and send him out. How's I gonna know?

Lord, I ain't wanna think about it no more. I seen how it is, in the aftermath. How everyone be looking for the piece of the thing that they woulda done different. I always hold myself above such mess. Ain't no use in wishful thinking. That kinda brain wringing don't come to no good. But all I'm thinking now . . . please stop me, Lord! All I'm thinking is how I's the one that set him to dusting.

I can't see nothing wrong with it, either. House needed dusting. Boy was there. Been home all afternoon, just loafing and goofing, not a care in the world. You give a boy like that a chore. That's what you do. Every time.

Lord, have mercy.

I been around a long time. I lost a lot of people I love. Can't stop myself loving, can't stop myself losing 'em. My own ma and pops, years back. Older brother, younger sister. Handful of nephews, that sort of thing. My big son, sick with the throat cancer.

It's a long time I been loving folk. Long time, I been losing 'em. But I ain't ever known a sorrow like this one.

BRICK

Damn right Tariq was wearing red and black. Like any good King. Straight up.

It's about time too. I've been ragging on him for two years. He was gonna be my lieutenant when the time was right. We both knew it. And time was coming due.

We knew it since we was little, way back when I became lieutenant to Sciss. We knew it was gonna be handed to me one day, and then to Tariq. We used to stand out back of the church, or over in the playground, and talk shit about Sciss and how much better and stronger the Kings would be when we was in charge. Straight up.

But you can't walk into the job fresh off. You got to choose the life and then you got to rise through the ranks. I gave Tariq the same advice Sciss once gave me: Don't come till you're ready, and then come all in. T was ready. He proved that last night on the sidewalk. He was ready.

TYRELL

No, no, no, no, is all I come up thinking. Hell, no. Tariq wasn't in the Kings.

They wanted him, of course. The 8-5s wanted him bad, but Tariq knew how to lay them off.

Brick would come around, pressing it, and Tariq would get into it with him. All the time. He was the only one of us I knew who could stand up to Brick and his guys like that.

The Kings are in everything. It's real hard to get out of the neighborhood without their stink on you. But it's what I want to do. And I got lucky, because that's what Tariq wanted, too. So we were in it together. Well, out of it together, I mean.

I don't know why anyone would think that Tariq was a King. I've seen him push it off a hundred times. When Brick and his guys come around—around the few of us who aren't already in, I mean—you have to act just right. You have to play it cool. They want to lean on you, make it sound real good to be up in something where a bunch of tough guys always have your back. They remind you how rough the neighborhood can get, and they promise to protect you. They'll teach you to fight so you don't have to walk afraid—of the Stingers, of the cops, of the random crazies who go around making trouble. They promise you cash, and spin it so good you get stars in your eyes.

Even when you know it's dead-end wrong, it all sounds so

right and so safe. You got to learn to blow them off without pissing them off, and Tariq had the magic touch.

I got real lucky. Tariq made it so I could keep my head down and just do my thing. Brick knew to lay off me, too, or Tariq would be in his face.

But Tariq's gone now.

REVEREND ALABASTER SLOAN

The plane hasn't even taken off before I flag down the flight attendant, ask for something to drink. She brings me a large scotch and soda, on the house. Celebrity has its perks.

I'm not afraid to fly, nor to enter a fresh media hoopla. No rule says I have to weigh in on the Tariq Johnson story; I brought this on myself. It's going to make national news, soon enough, and I want to be there when it does.

Yet my stomach is in knots. I can't even find a way to pray about it, because I can't stop thinking, *I wished for this.*

I was thinking just the other day that my campaign's been lagging. I needed some magic potion, some pick-me-up to bring me back into the spotlight. An issue to tout, a side to stand on, a moral high ground to stomp with my righteous foot. Ask and ye shall be granted, God says. *What have I done, Lord? This time.*

Tariq Johnson is dead, and I wished for it. Not for his death, specifically, but for something a whole lot like it. I have sinned.

I believe that I have been chosen. Tapped by the hand of God to bring my particular skills to bear on the issues facing blacks in America. I believe in God, that He works in mysterious ways . . . but this, this is too much.

The first-class seat cushion absorbs my weight as the plane takes off, bound for the small city that will soon be in the spotlight. I shut my eyes, try not to think it: *I wished for this.*

JENNICA

I put on my waitress uniform, the short, tight cream-colored dress and the ironed brown apron. I have to really suck it in to get it buttoned these days. I went for one a size too small. Better tips, I've learned, if the fabric hugs your hips and your cleavage crests between the buttons. It makes sense, I think, when I look at myself in the mirror.

Emmy offered to work for me today, but I said no, I can handle it. I can't take a day off and be sad, not when there's bills to pay at home. My aunt works hard just to keep a roof over our heads, so I chip in as much as I can to help out with everything else. I don't want to be a burden to her.

Noodle picks me up and drives me over to the diner, like usual. He has a real old car, one that he fixes up himself to keep it running. It has a bench seat. I slide in, all the way across so I'm sitting next to him. We don't talk in the car, though, which is strange.

"You okay?" he says at the third stoplight, all soft. He has his arm around my shoulders, across the bench seat back. His fingertips brush my biceps, and I feel like crying. When he's not around the Kings, he can be real thoughtful.

"Sure," I say. Maybe he'll believe me. Maybe he'll never need to know that there's a tiny mirror in my head, a memory screen showing Tariq's body beneath my hands, dying over and over again.

"They're planning a service for him, I heard. You wanna go to that?"

"Yeah."

"Okay, so we'll go," Noodle says. I rest my head on his shoulder, leave it there until we pull up at the diner.

"I love you," he says, which makes me feel warm.

"Love you, too," I respond, wishing I felt it the way he does. But it's just what you say, isn't it? To the guy you let kiss you and touch you all over. "You'll pick me up tonight?"

"Yeah."

"Can it be just us after that?" I ask.

"Okay," he says. "I mean, once we see Brick and them for a while."

I grit my teeth. *Of course.* I want to say, "Don't pick me up, then," because I really want some distance from the whole mess of it. Everything to do with the Kings, and Tariq.

What I actually say is, "Okay." And I let him kiss me.

"See you soon," Noodle says.

I give him a tiny wave and go inside. I take over for Shelly. She hugs me, which is strange, and heads on home. The small diner is quiet. One customer right now, and old Cup working the grill. I'll work alone from three to five, then there'll be three of us to cover the dinner rush.

They've got the TV on, as always. It's mounted high above the counter. The one customer is the old guy who's always in here, in counter seat number four. He gazes up at the set with reddened, watery eyes, sipping coffee that I will now and again offer to warm. He's a good tipper, and the kind who looks in your eyes and not at your chest like most of the counter guys. Lone wolves and whatnot.

Some kind of news is on. The pretty news anchor—Tammy? Tonya? I like her hair, all pretty and almost white. It makes me touch my own hair, its thick wavy darkness, bound at the base of my neck for health code reasons. I wish I could toss it, like she does, and have it flow delicate and smooth.

The frame cuts away, just like that, to a photo of Tariq. I flinch. It's all I can do not to drop the carafe of coffee.

"Controversy over the shooting last night," the male anchor says. "Some witnesses say Johnson may not have been armed at all."

"That's right, Carl." The cool blonde fills the screen again. "Sources say that the alleged shooter, Jack Franklin, may have mistaken a Snickers bar for a deadly weapon."

"It's hard to imagine," Carl says. "Making that kind of mistake."

I feel sick to my stomach.

"And he was just sixteen," the blonde says. "Possibly a gang member, say police, though his family has come forward to refute that claim. It seems there are more questions than answers in this story, Carl."

"That's right, Tracy. It's such a sad thing . . ."

I check the old guy's coffee one more time, then go into the kitchen. I don't want to hear any more.

BRIAN TRELLIS

Six o'clock, local news. Every station's got a different version of the story.

Johnson had a gun. Johnson didn't have a gun.

Johnson robbed a store. Johnson was minding his own business.

Johnson was a member of the 8-5 Kings. Johnson was in the wrong place at the wrong time, wearing the wrong clothes.

I saw what I saw. I told the police what I saw—Johnson running from the scene of the crime. Someone shouted to me that he had a gun, like a warning, and I backed off. I believe he had one, sure enough. He had a hard look in his eye, and I've been around Underhill long enough to know a guy doesn't come by that kind of coldness so casual.

Six-thirty, national news: *. . . growing controversy surrounding the shooting death of sixteen-year-old Tariq Johnson . . .*

I had just looked away from him, from those cold eyes, when the first shot hit.

Next thing I saw was Jack Franklin. He looked at me, too. Looked me square in the eye. I can't shake it. Can't help wondering if he saved my life or made a huge mistake.

TYRELL

The realness starts to sink in, slow and still kind of unbelievable. My skin tingles like it's on fire. I sit on the rug in front of the couch, staring at the television. I know I'm going to have to turn it off before Dad gets home, which is any minute.

The news is on. I usually watch at this time, but today it makes me feel sick to my stomach, and I don't want to get that way in front of Dad. He'll go for the throat if he senses any kind of weakness.

"Tyrell?" Dad calls. I didn't even hear the door open. My fingers fumble for the remote, somewhere near me. On the screen, Tariq's face appears. I've been waiting for them to cycle back to the story.

Dad comes in from the kitchen. "Tyrell, did you hear me?" His tone says he's already called after me more than once. But it doesn't matter. I can't turn it off. Not now.

His work boots approach me. I don't need to look at his face to know why he's mad. I forgot about the vegetables Mom left out for me to chop. They're supposed to be done and ready by the time she gets home to cook dinner. He's going to grab me, rip into me, but I don't even care. I don't look away from the news report.

"Tyrell!"

"Shut up!" It's a bad thing to say to Dad, but it just comes out. His step falters. I never talk back to him. Not ever. I duck my head against my knees.

Dad comes around the TV to see what I'm watching.

"That's your friend, isn't it?" He stands by the arm of the couch, knees at the level of my head.

I look up at him. Tariq has been in this apartment a thousand times. Probably a hundred times in the past year alone. Two or three times a week means a hundred and four times minimum, up to a hundred and fifty-six. And I'm only really counting weekdays there, which means tack on another fifty or so for the times he stopped by on the weekends.

Dad's looking back at me, expecting me to say something. The numbers just whirl in my head.

"Yeah," I say. "That's Tariq. You know him."

"Tariq," he says, like he needs to be reminded. "Right—that gang member who got killed last night?"

"He wasn't a—"

Dad's voice rises over mine. "He's a friend of yours? What the hell are you doing hanging around people like that?"

My throat clenches, and I can't even answer him.

"God damn it, Tyrell." Dad stomps into the kitchen.

In my peripheral vision, the same still image of Tariq flashes, over and over.

5. THE VIGIL

ROSALITA

You can hear the women wailing all up and down the block. Mournful and high, cries like soaring birds.

I'm too old for tears. Old enough to see we're all caught up in a great big circle. Birth, life, death. I see the beauty in it all.

It's supposed to be natural. You wear yourself down until your heart stops beating. Until your chest no longer sees fit to rise. These kids, though. These guns. Their bullets, their little tubes of metal that fly up and down the block . . . that's nothing natural.

I can't blame the women for crying like gulls. Any young boy's death is a slice across the pristine circle. It is a tragedy.

When I hear them start up wailing, I go on down to the street, to walk with them. I take their supple young hands in mine, the backs of which wave like the ocean. Veins beneath a whisper-skin. I tuck their tear-streaked cheeks to my breast, to comfort. I am nothing if not a picture of the truth that life goes on. And on. And on.

They tell me they were his friends. Beautiful young women, their faces lined with the first of many sorrows. It is a thing I cannot erase from them, nor would I try. We are caught in the circle.

Come with us, they say. To the vigil.

I stroke their hair. They are so young. To keep vigil means to wait. To keep watch. But these babies, these beauties, have no idea what it means to wait. I walk with them.

There's a brick wall up, right over near where the shooting happened. It was all taped off for an hour or two, maybe through the night, but by the morning, all the yellow tape had come down, and people started leaving flowers and candles and so on lined up along the sidewalk like a tribute. Someone came along and hosed down the bloodstain, but you can still see it. Real faint. I'm ninety-four, but my eyes are still good enough to see that. It is the first time in my life I ever wished my body would act its age. I have come to the point, at long last, where I have seen too much.

MELODY

Ms. Rosalita tucks me against her, and we walk. *Shh*, she whispers. I can't help crying, though. T was something special. I can't help but remember that my first kiss came from him. Back when we were thirteen. It wasn't ever gonna be serious, though. I mean, it wasn't ever gonna be me and T, sitting in a tree or nothing, but we got some of the *k-i-s-s-i-n-g* done, all the same.

Someone's got to be your first, and T was a good choice. Not scary or nothing. Not the type to try and get his freak on if you just even act a tiny bit like you might like him. So it was good practice. Maybe for both of us. I wonder that from time to time. If he thought I was a good choice, too. I mean, we knew each other forever. It happened easy.

How it happened was, we was walking home from school together one day. We weren't alone or nothing. There was other people with us, but we ended up kinda hanging back. No real reason. No plan. Least, I didn't have a plan, and if T had one, he was being real bad about bringing it to happen. So, anyway, we was walking. Not saying nothing. I figured he looked good, so I said something dumb, like, "You look good." I just blurted it out, right in the middle of trying to think of something better to say.

Tariq was all like, "What?"

So I said, "Never mind."

A minute or two passed, while I was feeling like a dumbass.

Then T says, "You look good too."

Then we was walking even slower, until the people we was with disappeared around the next corner. Then we wasn't walking anymore, and T goes, "So . . ."

And I say, "Yeah . . ."

And then it just kinda happened. He kissed me, or I kissed him, or something in the middle of that, where we just kinda came together, and it was perfect for a few moments. We kissed on the lips, and then we kissed with tongue. I never did it before. I don't know if he had, but it seemed to go okay. He put his arms all up around me, real gentle. It was nice. I woulda done it again with him later, but the time just never seemed right. We would look at each other, kinda secret-like, from time to time, and I would think, *Maybe* . . . but there was always people around. It just never happened. I always thought someday it would again. But not now . . .

So that was it. A couple minutes, maybe. Then we kept on walking.

We was on Peach Street that day, down past the shops a little. It happened kinda close to where he died, I figure. That's a little bit weird to think about. We was down in front of that old brick wall, so maybe it was even on the very same spot. You don't stop to measure when you're too busy worrying about how your breath smells. It coulda been the same exact spot. Now I got that to wonder about, too.

Hard to stop wondering it. 'Cause T's gone now, and I kissed him on the mouth one time, and his lips felt warm.

WILL (AKA eMZee)

I slap hands with my homies. "Gotta jet." If I'm not back in time for dinner, Mom will have it out for me.

"Jet? Bet you keep it in your garage," one of them says. I roll my eyes. They're forever razzing me about Steve being so rich.

"Naw, that's where we keep the chopper," I answer, slugging him in the arm.

We all laugh. "Catch you later, dog," they chorus as I make my way down the street.

I don't know what it means when they tease me. We're supposed to be tight, but I've never had any of them over to Steve's place. They ain't asked, either. I don't know if they would want to come, or if it'd be like showing off. I mean, you push a button, and ice cubes jump out of the door on the fridge. You can get crushed ice or shaved ice, even, if you have that kind of preference when it comes to ice. What the heck is that about? And six TVs? It's embarrassing.

I guess I'm not quite one of the guys anymore, which isn't fair. It's not like I chose Steve for my mom. It wasn't my idea to move across town. I don't disapprove, when it comes right down to it. Steve's nice enough. He's going to pay for me to go to college, which is a pretty good deal. We get along. Which is to say, I keep my head down most of the time, and he doesn't bother me. But I didn't choose a life like his, with him. Mom did.

The singing surrounds me before I can come up from my

thoughts. I'm on Peach Street. There's a crowd gathering. A small old woman presses a flower into my hand. Everyone has them—they're throwing them forward, against the wall, a great mound of petaled beauty in honor of Tariq. I hold mine. The singing is soft and close and tearful. Everyone on the street gently sways. The people fold me in, and before I can breathe, I feel like a part of something. It's a feeling I don't want to let go of.

KIMBERLY

Peach Street is all crammed with people hugging and crying. I have to walk through it, but I try not to look. At the faces, the flowers, all surrounding the place where it must have happened.

There's nothing I'd want to leave in tribute to Tariq. I can barely find the will to be sad for him, which makes me sad all in itself. It's not that I think he deserved to get shot or anything; I'm just not really surprised it went down like that, the way he was always hanging with Brick and the Kings. It's kind of what you sign up for when you put on the colors. Isn't it?

The person I ache for is Tina, his sister, so small and probably so confused by what's happening.

I should go by and see her, maybe. I'm sure she'd remember me from when I used to babysit her. That seems like a good thing to do.

Everyone forgets about the smallest, most fragile ones when there's high drama going on. My daddy died when I was four, and it was all so strange and hectic and upsetting. All these extra people in the house, and everyone trying to hug me, and I didn't really understand why. I remember squeezing beneath a couch and hoping and praying that my dad would just come and get me. I knew he was dead, and I knew dead meant gone, but Daddy had been gone before and he always came back. I don't know how long it was before I realized that, this time, gone meant forever and always. Longer than I would ever admit.

So I kind of wonder . . . I wonder if Tina's sitting there, quietly waiting for Tariq to come home.

TINA

Songs float in the window.
A vigil, Nana says. *For Tariq.*
Mommy says, *No.*
I'm not going to look at the spot where he died.
Nana holds my hand, and we walk down Peach Street.
Flowers and candles and a whole crowd of people.
Nana says, *Look how much everyone loved Tariq.*
But no one loves Tariq as much as me.

REVEREND ALABASTER SLOAN

The young girl comes toward me, wielding a powder puff. She says her name is Kimberly. She's not a girl, but a woman, I suppose—she curves like a woman, at any rate—but that flawless smooth brown skin only reminds me that I'm getting on in years.

She has a wide open face, like a child, but her generous hip bumps against my thigh as she works to get me camera ready. Her brow furrows in concentration. Twenty years from now, she'll have wrinkles in those spots, but for now I can enjoy the view. My gaze drops down, down, past her full, parted lips to the column of throat to the barest hint of cleavage.

"No, look at the ceiling," she says, whisking the brush across my cheeks.

The ceiling is dimpled white, the familiar foam-board squares that always top off a grade school classroom.

"Sorry."

"You're fine," she says.

When my son was young, he got detention once for throwing paper airplanes at the ceiling during class. His mother had to go pick him up early. By way of explanation, he told her, "We were trying to get them to stick in the cracks." She related this to me later, still hopping mad. I laughed. "Well, did it work?" I asked her. She started to laugh, too. "He didn't say!" We never did find out. No good way to ask that of your kid when you're trying to punish him. I could ask him now, I suppose. It would give me a reason to call, other than simply to hear his voice and feel glad that something like this didn't happen to him. Because it could have.

"Do you want blush?" Kimberly asks.

"Do I need it?"

"Not really."

"Thank you for doing this." I caught the first flight down after the news broke. My staff thought it would be a good idea, but we're smack in the middle of the campaign, so not even my personal assistant came with me. The guy who usually touches up my makeup is back in DC, coordinating press releases about why I'm canceling my appearances there this week. My face on television, comforting Tariq Johnson's family, will draw more voters and more campaign contributions than any stuffy old dinner with rich people I could host. At least that's the theory.

"It's no problem," Kimberly says. "It makes me feel special."

"You're very special," I answer. "I can tell." It's the sort of thing women like to hear. It's also the sort of line that's gotten me in trouble before. All that smooth, young skin. Those wide eyes gazing at me like I'm something magical.

Her fingers whisk excess foundation from my jawline. I clear my throat and tug the napkin from my collar. On another day, perhaps. But not during the campaign. I ease off the stool. When I stand, we are no longer face-to-face.

"Okay," she says. "Wait—" She adjusts my collar, neatens up my tie. I raise my chin, let my eyes drift shut. Not during the campaign.

"You're better-looking in person." A tiny burst of sound. I open my eyes. "I always wondered," she adds. I glance down, catch the slight purple flush across her cheeks.

"Is that a compliment?" I'm not really sure.

"Yeah," she says. "I didn't mean you look bad on TV or anything." She has a great smile.

The campaign volunteer who drove me in from the airport pokes her head into the room. "The cameras are out front now," she says. "Five minutes." She bobs back into the hallway, immediately reabsorbed in her phone.

"Great. Now I just have to figure out what to say." This is for Kimberly's benefit. It's another thing people like to hear. Folks who meet me for the first time like to feel that they're being brought behind the scenes. You learn, over the years, how to please people. How you really are isn't important if you can pretend to be a person who pleases people.

In this case, I'm only half joking. No words can describe the sorrow I felt upon hearing the circumstances of Tariq Johnson's death, and none can convey my frustration with the system that allowed his killer to walk free. But I am, as ever, tamping down my feelings. Because how I feel shouldn't matter. I turn my attention toward how I must speak. All that matters is that I say the right thing—what people need to hear.

"I knew him," she says. "We went to the same church."

"You did?" I lift her hand, cup her small fingers, flirt with danger. "I'm very sorry."

Kimberly shrugs, clearly embarrassed to accept my condolences.

Her gaze drops to our hands, now linked. "I'm sorry for his mother," she says. "No one deserves a thing like this."

"No."

Tears stand in her eyes. "It's terrible, what happened," she says. "But I really didn't know him very well."

"Were you in school together too?"

"Oh, no." She half smiles. "I'm much older."

I wonder what constitutes "much" in her mind.

"Will it come to you?" she asks. "When you get in front of the cameras, will you just know what you want to say?"

"Maybe," I answer. Sometimes it happens that way. I can talk my way out of a paper bag, if need be. I'm a minister. A politician. I know how to do the dance. "What would you say?"

"I'm not sure," she murmurs. "I didn't know him very well."

She's being shy. I want to shake her, shake something loose. Some small tidbit of something personal about Tariq. Because in a moment I have to walk out there and, effectively, eulogize him. And I didn't know him at all.

And yet, I do know him, because I know a hundred, a thousand young black men, and it could have been any one of them shot. My own son . . . I press the emotion away. *Just think it, don't feel it*, I remind myself.

My thumbs stroke the soft skin of the young woman's hands. "Thank you, Kimberly. You've been a big help."

KIMBERLY

I couldn't tell the whole truth to someone like Alabaster Sloan. I knew Tariq, and I know his mama and his sister and his greatma. I knew him, sure enough, but the whole truth is that I hated him.

My first job babysitting was for Tariq and Tina. Tina's always been a sweet girl, real quiet and simple. But Tariq . . . in my head I still think of him as terror boy.

I never wanted to go over there, because of him. But my mama told me, *Never turn down a handful of money for a few hours' easy work.* I couldn't explain to her why it wasn't so easy. I was supposed to be able to handle those kids. I should have been able to, and most of the time I could get them to mind, but Tariq had a mouth like a sledgehammer.

I already knew him from church before I ever stepped foot in his house. He and his friends called me Fat Face. They picked up on it from a boy in my grade called Brick. They all looked up to Brick. I guess he came off to them as cool, being so much older. He was a real punk, twisted in the brain, but the little boys never could see that.

Brick loved to torment me something fierce. He'd call me Fat Face, blow out his cheeks, and do a little dance making fun of the parts of me that tend wide. I knew I was big, but for the most part, I thought that was okay.

My hips came in early, is how it started. Guys around the neighborhood would whistle when I walked by. I would hear them talking about how I looked fine, how they wanted to break my cherry. I pretended not to listen. It made me feel weird, that they were looking so close, but it made me feel good, too, because I could tell they were liking what they saw.

Then Brick started in. I don't even know why. I never did anything to him. *Fat Face. Hippo Hips*, he would say. *Here comes the blimp.* He'd walk around me, staring, acting all puzzled, till Tariq or someone would ask him what he was doing, and he'd say he was looking for the strings that were holding me down.

I wish it was Brick who got shot. I'm not ashamed to wish it, either.

Tariq and his friends would be all clustered around Brick, watching his every move. They rolled their jackets like him when that was the thing, wore combs in their hair when he did. But Tariq liked to think himself a wordsmith, so it all got worse after they started hanging around. Brick's arsenal of insults was small. Same thing, day in, day out. Fat Face. Hippo Hips. Blimp. He thought he was so damn clever.

I figured out how to deal with it. Figured it would pass. But when the shit got old, Tariq would come up with some new way to mess with me. He tried to jump on my back one day. Called it the elephant ride. Got them all doing it. I had to go to the doctor the week after; my back was hurting real bad from all the strain. Things like that.

I hated them. I used to look at myself in the mirror and try to see what was so fat about my face. Mama says that's just its shape: round.

When Brick got busy with the 8-5 Kings, he laid off me. Tariq and his friends, not so much. Tariq got a little bit nicer later, I guess. He got nice enough to ignore me instead of making up new jokes, and the old ones slowly died. I finished school, got my haircutting license, and got a job at Mollie's Manes. It pays well, and I like it.

Today, I get to put makeup on Alabaster Sloan. I'm standing a couple of inches from him, with my hands on his skin. That makes me as close to being a celebrity as we have in this town. I'll be telling this story around the salon for years to come. And I guess I have Tariq to thank for it. Wow, that's such a bitchy thought. So wrong. *Thanks for dying, Tariq, so I could get my fifteen minutes of fame.*

I can't help feeling a little bit glad about it. I mean, I'm not glad he's dead or anything. Honestly. I'm not hateful like that. I have mean thoughts sometimes, because I can't help the things that pop into my head, but I don't want to be like that. Yet here I am, alone in a room with Alabaster Sloan, close enough to touch. Actually touching. How else was something that amazing ever going to happen to someone like me?

In person, he seems quieter, less brusque. On camera he's a take-charge, my-words-will-blow-you-down, blustering powerhouse of a man. He seems larger than life. Up close, he's not much bigger than I am. Taller, but slim. There's a softness about him that surprises me. His eyes move around the room, and when they rest on me, I feel like he is looking deep.

Lots of people look at me, but no one looks at me deep. Guys still whistle when I walk down the street. *Do you want some fries to go with that shake?*

They grind against me uninvited when I go dancing with my friends. Strange hands at my waist. *Yeah, baby, back that ass up.*

I've never had a guy who's interested in the rest of me. One who likes to look into my eyes. To most guys, I'm just a round face, a double-E cup, a pair of hippo hips.

That's why, when the reverend takes hold of my hand, I let him. When his lips brush the back of my knuckles, I think, *He likes me enough to kiss me.*

He asks me what I would say to all those cameras if I was him. Then he stops and waits. Tilts his head as if he's really ready to listen to what I have to say.

It's a crazy thing to do. Completely crazy. He's a celebrity. Someone I've seen on television. Say his name to anyone, they'll go, "Yeah, I heard of him." He's married, too. But he's in the room, and he's looking at me all soft . . .

I stretch my round self upward. Kiss him on the lips.

TOM ARLEN

It's always sad when a kid dies. I've lived here twenty years, and I've seen more than my fair share of funeral processions. I don't understand the violence. The way these young men run around the neighborhood, acting like they're so tough. Then when one of them dies, they answer by killing some more.

Plenty of deaths and other rough crimes around here, but I've never seen Underhill on national news before. Can't think of a time, anyway. And I'm not sure what's all that different in this case. Two guys with guns, one dies—it's an everyday story. I have a month's worth of local newspapers gathered up in my recycling bags, and I bet I could find five stories that read about the same. Two guys with guns. Except one thing—in all those other stories, I bet anything, both parties were black. They're out to get Jack Franklin because he's white.

They're calling him a racist, a murderer. But anyone would stand up in the face of a gun. That's just common sense. How is it racist?

Jack's lucky, is all. He got his shot off first. If Tariq had fired first, Jack would be just another victim of gang violence. Certainly not worth this media circus. They'd all shake their heads and put him in the ground, and the world would keep on spinning.

Reverend Sloan came down from Washington, it looks like. There he is, on the TV, standing right down the block on Peach Street, in the middle of this vigil. Poaching some limelight off a poor dead black boy and the hand of the white man who put him there. The nerve of some people. Politicians especially. Everything is about scoring polling points, even if the shots are cheap.

I'm about to turn it off and go outside to see it for myself, but what's Sloan talking about now?

What the hell is this, about a Snickers bar being mistaken for a gun? I saw that gun plain as day. And it was pointed right at Jack Franklin.

JUNIOR

Guys on my cell block are all worked up over some shooting what happened down in Underhill. I try to keep to myself when there's hoopla, but some of them know it's my 'hood, so they're coming by to find out my opinion.

I just tell them I don't know. Stop short of telling them I don't care, because they're pretty upset. Best I can tell, some brother got smoked by some whitey, who's gonna walk. So what else is new?

"Man, that's your 'hood," the guys say. "That's your colors. Whatta you gotta say about it?"

I don't care about much of anything to do with where I used to call home. Once a King, always a King, sure. I carry that, but this is home now. For life. Can't waste time thinking about it any other way.

It's interesting, though, because not that much from outside gets these guys riled up. Someone's always getting shot somewhere. What makes this one so different? As if we don't have enough problems with factions on the inside, we need to worry about what's happening on the street?

I go out and look at the TV. It's high in a box, behind mesh and wire in the corner of the rec room.

Great. It's that preacher, Sloan.

That blowhard thinks he's all that because he threw a Molotov cocktail once, back in the nineties in some kind of race riot. Turned his life around after. Around to what? Wearing a nice suit and sucking up to reporters? I wear a suit too. I got people to suck up to.

I nod to one of the guards.

"Hey, Junior," he says. "What do you think about all this?"

On the outside, I never woulda thought of myself as the kind of guy who everybody wants an opinion from. I always just kinda did what other people were doing.

I don't care what's going down outside. Why should I weigh in?

Except . . . that's Tariq on the TV. That's Tariq Johnson.

Now I'm pulling up a chair.

STEVE CONNERS

Will comes home forty-five minutes late, carrying a wilted white carnation. He slides in the door, real quiet-like. Sees me and jumps about a mile.

Obviously, he wasn't expecting me to be sitting right there in the foyer, waiting.

"You're pretty late. Where have you been?" I ask him. Keep it conversational. I don't see it as my place to discipline my stepson. And I've never had cause to. Will's a pretty good kid. Exceptionally good, I'd say, based on the guys I used to know at his age and the things I see on TV. Will's the kind of kid I was, always keeping his nose clean. Bright future ahead of him.

"Where's Mom?" he says, instead of answering.

His mother isn't home yet, because of a work emergency. Which is lucky, I suppose, because she'd be beside herself. The Tariq Johnson shooting has really gotten under her skin.

She called me at the office this afternoon, crying. She'd seen the mother on TV, being ushered out of the city mortuary where she'd gone to make arrangements for the burial of her son. I saw that coverage. The mother made no comments to the media, but an uncle had spoken: *Tariq was a good student and an upstanding citizen. He was unaffiliated with any street gang, and we are confident he was unarmed and innocent of the charges being leveled against him. Jack Franklin shot an innocent child.*

"Your mom's stuck at work," I tell Will. His eyes brighten a little. He knows he lucked out. "Where were you?"

He tucks the carnation behind his back, like a guilty secret. "Nowhere."

Last place I saw carnations? On TV. Spread in a blurry mountain across the face of the makeshift shrine at Tariq Johnson's murder site.

"Have you been down to Underhill?" I ask, though it seems inconceivable. It's all the way across town. He'd have had to ride the bus for an hour.

"Don't tell my mom," he says. "You don't have to tell her I was late. Please."

"You shouldn't be going down there." My voice is harsh enough to make him flinch. "It's dangerous. Especially at night."

"Not for me," Will says. "I'm from there."

"So was the Johnson boy," I retort. "It's too dangerous." It's not my place to scold or discipline him. But the angry words keep coming. "What were you thinking? You stay away from there, you hear me?" The shaky fear that overtakes me makes no sense.

"I wanted to pay my respects," he shouts. "Nothing wrong with that. Those are my friends."

I take a breath. "Did you know the Johnson boy?" It's hard to realize, but it's possible. Will grew up in Underhill. They could have been friends, long ago. But Will should be putting that past behind him. He's not stuck in a bad part of town anymore. I'm giving him every opportunity he could ever imagine.

"I ain't have to know him to know him," Will says.

He uses that word on purpose, knowing it rubs me the wrong way. "Use your language properly," I remind him. "You're better than that."

"I ain't no better than Tariq," he says, storming past me. "And neither are you."

REVEREND ALABASTER SLOAN

After all the clamor at the vigil—the clicking of cameras, the flashes of light, the shouted questions—the hotel room is starkly quiet. Always a profound relief. The door whooshes shut behind me, DO NOT DISTURB. I drop to my knees, beg the forgiveness of the most high God.

I prayed for this.

I prayed for something to happen.

Politically, this can only help me, no matter which way anything goes. I couldn't have dreamed up a scenario more perfect. This terrible ordeal answers my prayers.

It was easy, sitting in my office in Washington, to think of Tariq Johnson as a statistic. To think of his story as political fodder, and I'm ashamed of that to begin with, but when I stand down here, and hold his grandmother's hand, the world inverts. When I join in the singing, listen to the crying. When people reach out to me to lead, it is no longer a story on paper. I can taste the tears behind every sound bite. I fall under the cloak of grief as well. It is real to me now.

Who have I become, Lord, that I can find distance enough to pray for such tragedy?

I've been faulty.

I have learned my lesson.

Lord Jesus, I have learned my lesson.

SAMMY

The vigil is never gonna end, I think. Two blocks away, and I can hear the goddamn singing. Dumbass people. There's no cause for a lullaby. Tariq's already asleep.

The whole neighborhood's quieter than usual. This street, Onerfin Avenue, is the line between our territory and the start of Stinger turf. On our side of the O, we deal weed. On their side, you can get your coke. If you're into that, which plenty of people are.

Onerfin's usually humming, even late. On a good night, we'd be talking fifteen, twenty sales by now. I've turned over three packs of product so far, and that's it.

Car-radio music thumps from about a block away. I live through a couple tense seconds before it turns the corner and I know if it's Kings or Stingers rolling by. It's them. On their own side, at least.

The O is a four-lane road, plus parking on both sides, which leaves a good amount of space between the Stingers and us, but we can see each other across the way.

On our side we run what we call a hydrant roll. I'm the money man, first stop. Someone drives up in their car, pulls to the hydrant, and lowers the window. They tell me what they want, pay me, and I walkie-talkie it to the guy at the next hydrant, who supplies the product. Car pulls down there for pickup. It's a lot of responsibility. I gotta be able to judge if someone might be a cop and be able to refuse the sale. I gotta know all the prices cold and do the math right. I'm accountable for all the cash of an evening. That's why I need a piece. If someone tries to roll me or my product man, I'll be all over it.

I got my piece in my pocket now. Keeping watch, as usual, on the line. It's a different kind of vigil. One that ain't gonna end when people start to forget about Tariq.

Not me, though. I won't forget. We go too far back. T's got fingers in my brain, gripping tight. Death grip, I guess. Too tight to ever let go.

We grew up together. We were tight like a knot in an old rope, me and Junior, Tyrell and Tariq. Four musketeers. Nothing beats that way-back history. Not even the Kings. I woulda lay down for T way before I would for Brick or any of those guys.

I let T down, though. I saw Jack Franklin coming. Saw his gun and didn't move fast enough. Didn't get the gun in my hand in time. I coulda shot him dead. Coulda stopped the whole thing.

How come I froze when it counted? I ain't froze now. I'm steamed.

My blood heats easy tonight, each time the Stingers roll by. I wish Jack Franklin was a friggin' yellow jacket. If they had killed Tariq, I could do anything I want as retribution. But there's no one to lash out at. If I step off my sidewalk and pull my piece, yeah, it'll feel good, but it'll be war. A big mess, and T wasn't about that.

I pull the piece into my hand anyway. Look upon its gleaming black skin. I guess I should get some polish for it. Some nice new bullets. Or maybe trade it in for a long gun. A rifle. Something with a scope. I'm in the mood to do a little hunting.

The guy, Jack Franklin—the cops just let him go. He's out there somewhere. Probably thinks he's untouchable.

6. SNICKERS

EDWIN "ROCKY" FRY

By dawn, all that's left of the vigil is a pile of flowers, some wrapped in bundles, some tossed alone. Their soft scent covers the hard truth of what has happened here.

I hurry past, skirting the sprawling mound. Wind rustles the flowers' plastic wrapping. The strangest thing is knowing I wrapped many of those myself, right in my store a few days ago. Last night I sold out of carnation and wildflower bundles well before dark. I had to put in a special order to replace them.

I sell these things, yet I almost never know where they end up. When a young man buys a five-dollar bouquet, is it for his sweetheart, a sick friend, his mother? It's rarely worth my energy to wonder.

Bales of newspapers await me. As I lay them out on the racks,

I peel the top one off each stack. It's my morning routine, yet today it carries more weight than ever before. I start the coffee machines, then settle on my stool behind the counter to read.

REV. SLOAN ARRIVES IN UNDERHILL: CANDLELIGHT VIGIL HONORS MURDERED TEEN

Guilt settles over my shoulders. The story of Tariq's death unfolds and unfolds, and with each new crease, I can see my place in it.

Someone told the cops how I was yelling after Tariq. *Stop thief*, they thought I was saying.

That wasn't it at all.

POLICE EVIDENCE LOG CONFIRMS: JOHNSON WAS UNARMED

I didn't have to go out there. I could've stayed inside, minding my business. Tariq's momma would've sent him back sooner or later.

I always try to mind my own business. People come in, they buy what they want. They pay, I make change. It's very straightforward. Most people who bust out the door without waiting for change, I keep it. Their loss, right? I'll set it aside for the day in case they come back, sure—beyond that, it's not my problem. But I knew Tariq; he'd been coming into my store since he was a kid. His momma's good people. So I went after him. I was just trying to help.

A NEW CITIZEN POLICE FORCE?
EYEWITNESSES RECOUNT COURAGEOUS ACTION
BY ARMED CITIZEN

Johnson had a gun, this article insists. Another declares, *Actually, it was a Snickers bar.*

Maybe he did have a gun—I just didn't see it. Maybe that's so. I can't testify to it, but it's what I want to believe. Better that than the alternative. An unimaginable mistake over some candy Tariq bought here, from me.

BRICK

Nowadays it's all over the TV, how Tariq didn't even have a gun.

Bullshit. I was there. I saw it go down. I saw the gun in Tariq's hand. I remember it clear as day.

It was black. A quality piece. Firepower like that's no kind of a joke. I saw it. I saw it, and I knew: T was finally coming around.

Where's the gun now? they're all asking. Talking about a Snickers bar instead. Ain't no one gonna confuse a Snickers bar for a weapon. I wouldn't, anyway. I know a piece when I see one.

Where's the gun now? I'll tell you where. One of my boys musta picked it up and pocketed it. That's a nice piece. You don't let shit like that go to waste in some evidence locker. Hell, no.

If I'd been the closest to Tariq, I'd have pocketed it. For sure. One of my boys musta got it, Sammy or Noodle or . . . I don't know. When I figure out who, he's gonna have to give it to me. And then I'm gonna cut him for not giving it over to me right away.

VERNESHA

The tiny children line up to get on the school bus. They are barely as tall as the tires. Their backpacks hang off them like potato sacks, all lumpy and jouncing on the backs of their knees.

Tariq was once small like that. He went off to school. I sent him out into the big bad world alone.

I didn't worry enough.

That was my job: to worry, and to keep him safe. But Tariq was always so strong, so easy.

I worry plenty about Tina. Half a dozen different doctors, all with a different story. Every test costs money, and in the end, I'm not looking for a cure—just a way to understand what's going on in her head. Mom's always saying, *Some people are just simple. That baby's gonna be fine.*

When Tina came along, that's where all my fretting went, I guess.

Other mothers worried more. About the gangs, and the drugs, and the police, and the violence.

Tariq was going to be fine. I didn't worry nearly enough.

WILL (AKA eMZee)

I never think anything of wearing my hoodie. Throw it on, go outside. It's what people wear, you know? You gotta have a hoodie to fit in. Let your pants hang low. Like the other guys.

My mom and Steve want me to be wearing all the preppy clothes, the khakis and the polo shirts with the collar and what-not. But I can't be seen fronting that. My grades are too good. I already have to worry about making my speech sound street when I'm out, and making it sound proper when I'm home. My mom's all proud of me for being smart, but most of my homies don't know I'm on the honor roll. I can't be going around dressed like a geek, or they'll catch on.

I'm pissed about what happened to Tariq—there's enough around here to be scared about without having to be scared about how I dress. Now I got another thing to juggle. I hardly get any sleep as it is, because I have to hang with the guys in Underhill after school while my mom thinks I'm at the library, then I come home and do my homework after dinner or on the bus, and then go back out to tag once she thinks I've gone off to bed.

But my mom took away all my hoodies last night. Says I have to make do without them, so I won't get shot. I tried to tell her I'm not gonna be stupid like Tariq was, running around with the hood up, sporting colors. She took them anyway. Then she cried. I gave her a hug and all, but in the morning I went down to the corner and paid this guy from school to lend me one of his old hoodies, just until the heat wears off the Tariq situation and my mom relaxes. I know how much she loves me, but she doesn't understand. I gotta fit in if I want to survive.

TYRELL

I keep thinking back on shit that happened a long time ago. Dumb shit, too, like how pissed I was at Tariq for stealing the nickname T before I could get to it. I was so damn mad over that, I remember. It was kind of a phase we went through, where everyone was called by their initial. Sammy was S, Junior was J, and Tariq became T.

T became T immediately, before I even got a chance to try it out. Everyone just started calling him that. I didn't think it was fair. And no one seemed to notice it except me. So we'd be walking down the street and other guys would be like, "Yo, S. Yo, J. Yo, T. Yo, Tyrell."

I threw a punch at T one time over it. Way back, when the initial thing was new. He just walked up to me and was like, "Tyrell—" and I hauled off and punched him. It happened out of the blue, for both of us.

His nose started bleeding. I covered my head in case he decided to hit me back. But he just grabbed his face and said, "Shit, man."

So I said, "Sorry."

"What gives?"

"How come you get to go by T?" I said. Really, I think it was a whole stew of things that had me feeling roughed up that day— stuff from home, stuff from school. But some things were fixable, and some things weren't.

"Well, it starts my name . . . ?" he said slowly. He pulled up his shirt and dabbed his face with it.

"Mine too."

T cleaned himself up best he could with us standing on the stoop. "You can be T," he said. "Is that what you want?"

I didn't know what I wanted. I sat down and put my head on my arms. T sat down next to me. "Ty, my man," he goes. "You so much bigger than one letter."

After that, he started calling me Ty. Other guys picked up on it. It made me feel good. I got a nickname like the others, but it was bigger, like T said.

That was years ago. New shit happened, and I forgot all about that punch. Sammy became Sammy again. Junior became Junior again, which frankly was a nickname in the first place. But I'm still called Ty to this day, and T stayed T, for some reason.

TINA

The phone rings and rings and rings.

Not usual.

Tariq's bedroom door is closed and locked.

Not usual.

The counters and the tables and the kitchen chairs are covered
with baskets and platters and foil pans and plastic cartons of
food.

I can eat anything I want.

Not usual.

There's fruits and crackers and cheeses and cakes and noodles
and weird-looking salads and chicken and pie and potatoes and
macaroni.

I open them all and nobody yells.

Yummy.

But not usual.

The phone rings and rings and rings and rings and rings and
rings and rings.

Mommy picks it up and throws it, *crack*, against the wall.

It's quiet in the house.

Very, very unusual.

REVEREND ALABASTER SLOAN

Vernesha sits with fingers knotted together. I have sat with a hundred grieving women, and this is what they do. Sit quietly with folded hands while the world rips their sons, husbands, sisters, loved ones to shreds. I wonder if the power of their own hands holds them together.

She follows my gaze to the lump of shattered plastic and metal on the floor beneath the window. "They won't stop calling."

She wears a half smile. I can't imagine where it comes from in the midst of the tornado she's standing in.

"No, they won't stop," I tell her. "Sometimes the best thing to do is to get out in front of it."

She nods, distant. "I want to speak."

"It's smart to have Marvin doing the talking right now." Vernesha's brother has made some statements, defending Tariq's character and decrying the general wrongness of how this whole thing went down. "He's making sure your voice is being heard, but it's quite soon for anyone to expect you to speak. And I'm here now." As if that's any reassurance. "I made one statement on my way in here, and I'll be holding a press conference in a couple of hours."

"I'll come," she says, squeezing her fingers tighter. "I want to speak."

I have known in my life but a shred of the power of women's

hands. For a moment, I feel as if Tariq himself is folded between her palms, unable to slip away.

"You don't have to."

Her eyes turn sharp. Dangerous. "I have to. I'm his mother."

"Well, you can't really go wrong," I tell her, stopping short of the truth: *Whatever you do, they'll eat it up.*

The little sister comes out. "You're on TV," she says. "Reverend Alabaster Sloan." She pronounces every syllable. *Rev-er-end Al-a-bas-ter Sloan.* "Civil rights activist and senatorial candidate." She parrots the byline they typically run beneath my face.

"Hello, Tina." I haven't inquired about her condition. It seems beside the point. She's charming, more so with each curious peek into the room.

"You're on TV."

"Yes, you would have seen me on TV." *And soon you'll be on there too.* I put out my hand, to shake. Tina gazes disdainfully at my open palm.

"Be polite," her mother says.

Tina shakes her head. "You're on TV. Do you want to see?"

"Are you watching the news channel?" her mother says.

The little girl twists her hands. She becomes a small shadow of her mother, yet it's hard to know whether she really understands the situation. "Nana is."

"Mom, for heaven's sake!" Vernesha calls. She plucks a few crumbs off Tina's shirt. "Go tell Nana it's time for your cartoons."

"It's not time," Tina says. "Twenty more minutes."

"Watch something else until then, okay?" Vernesha turns back to me. "I want to speak," she repeats. "I want them reporting the truth about Tariq. Not these lies."

"All right." Secretly, I'm glad. Secretly, this is why I came here.

"Whatever I have to do," she says. "Just tell me."

I admire women like this. I don't know where they get the strength.

REDEEMA

I cut the volume low. I need to know what they's saying about our boy. I know Vernesha don't want Tina watching this. I don't either. But it's the only TV, and I gotta know what they's saying. I got a right to know.

I send Tina off. "Go on to your room." She'll come right back, though, like one of them spinning tops. The harder you set it off, the faster it spins back at you.

It's the same with anything you try to push away. That's why I keep on watching the news, although I'd rather shut it off and look after my babies. But I gotta know what they's talking about, so it don't sneak up and hit us.

TOM ARLEN

Doorbell rings. It's the last person I'd expect to see standing on my stoop today. I grab his arm. "Get inside." I glance up and down the street before I slam the door. "What the hell are you doing here? If the Kings catch you, they're liable to knife you."

"I have protection," he says, patting the holster at his hip.

"Jesus Christ." I'm eyeing the gun now. A gun that killed a boy. Now it's under my roof. "They didn't take it?"

"Yeah, they took it when they brought me in," he says. "But I got it back."

He follows me into the living room, and I pour us a couple of drinks. I turned off the news coverage when I went to answer the door. Good thinking, it turns out.

"Look, can I stay here for a couple of nights?" he asks.

I'm shocked. "You want to stay in Underhill?"

"I can't go home," he says. "My lawyer says not to talk to any reporters, but they're camped outside my house. They're shining lights in my fucking windows, trying to see if I'm there. I don't think I could even get in; they'd swamp me."

"The reporters come by here, too. I'm a witness on record. They know you borrowed my car."

"Thanks for going on record, by the way. Lawyer says it helped me out. I told them self-defense right away, but they still questioned me. They said they had some conflicting statements, but they never made it sound like a big deal. I didn't know the whole world was gonna come after me." He chuckles, but I hear the nerves underneath.

We sip drinks, and he tells me his story. Being hauled downtown, questioned, released with no charges pending. I'm interested in how it all happened, of course. Lived here twenty years, and I've never known a gunman in Underhill to walk away that easy, no matter the circumstances.

"You know I can't go back out there," he says. "Not till things cool off."

"Well, sure, you're welcome to stay, pal." Though I can think of a dozen reasons why it's a bad idea. Reporters. Kings. Damned inconvenient.

JENNICA

That Reverend Sloan is on the news again. He's not even from here, but he's quickly becoming the face of this thing. It's so weird.

"Jen, can I get some more coffee?" says the regular at the end of the counter. His name is Cliff. Heathcliff, actually. He told me that one time.

It came up because he noticed I had changed my name. My name tag says Jen. J-E-N in big block letters that come on stickers. They have rolls of stickers in the back, different sizes because some people's names are longer than others'. You have to make your own tag. Mine used to say Jennica, but I changed it after the first month. People always wanted to strike up conversation about it. *Oh, that's pretty*, and so forth. Especially some of the jerks who come in and think I'm into them because I smile and bring them food. Like they don't even get that it's my job; they think I'm doing it for fun or something, like I'm doing something special just for them. The manager wouldn't give me a new name tag unless I paid for it, so I had to peel off the last four stickers and scrape off all the gum. It was worth it.

Going to work is like playing a role now. It makes it easier to pretend that "Jennica" can someday be something more.

I warm Cliff's coffee. I usually try to stay on top of it without him having to ask. But it's the kind of day where all I can do is stare at the TV screen or out at the street and try to put the two together. The whole picture of what's happened to Tariq. I blink and blink, but it doesn't gel.

The bells above the door jangle. A man and a woman come in. She has a tan satchel over her shoulder and a notepad in her hand. He has a video camera on his shoulder hefted with one hand while he uses the other to open the door for her. I automatically reach for two menus, although right away I can see this is going to be something else.

The woman smiles, showing perfect teeth. "Hello, Miss Brewer?" She's a breezy blonde with a ponytail and a smooth voice.

"Yes."

"Do you mind if I ask you a few questions? I understand you were present when Tariq Johnson was shot."

"I'm at work," I say. "I can't talk to you now."

"It would just take a minute. We're putting together footage for tonight's news."

"It's not time for my break. I can only talk to paying customers." I hear myself say it, like a robot voice from the back of my head. My lips feel dry. Immobile.

The woman's ponytail swings as she takes a seat at the counter, at the opposite end from Cliff. The cameraman doesn't sit, he just moves to stand closer behind her. I stare into the lens. It's both black and clear, a giant unblinking eye.

"I'll have some coffee, then," she says. Her wallet comes out. I glimpse a wad of green bills that seems unfairly thick. She lays a crisp, flat twenty on the table. "This should cover it."

I have no choice but to set a mug and saucer in front of her. The coffee steam rises as I pour. I used to enjoy the smell. Now I'm immune. "Can I get you anything else?"

"I'd just like to ask you a few questions," she says. The cameraman already has the camera on his shoulder, the lens glaring right into my face.

"I really have to work."

Two more twenties appear.

"I don't have anything interesting to say," I tell her.

"I'm sure that's not true." She extracts two more.

At this point I'm looking at all the money I'm going to make this shift, doubled. I take the stack, fold it into the tips pouch on my apron. The woman swirls one finger in the air in a circle motion. A light on the camera blinks on, blinding me.

"Where were you when it happened?"

"Across the street. We were just minding our own business and then we heard the shots."

"We?"

"My boyfriend and I."

"What's your boyfriend's name?"

I shift my feet. "Do I have to say that?" Noodle wouldn't like it.

"Well, it would—"

"No," Cliff says, from down the counter. "You don't have to say anything you don't want to."

The reporter glares at him. "Please go on, Miss Brewer. What happened next?"

"After he was shot?"

"Yes."

"The guy got in his car and drove off."

"The alleged shooter, Jack Franklin?"

"Yes. And Tariq was just lying there." I can see him now, in my mind's eye.

"It must have been awful," the reporter says softly.

"It was," I say. "I tried to save him. You know, CPR. But there was a lot of blood. They told me later he was gone right away. There was nothing I could do."

"Still. You must be very brave," she says.

"I don't know about that."

"Do you think Jack Franklin should be prosecuted?"

Yes. I shrug. "I don't know about those things."

"Surely you have an opinion, though? Having seen what you saw."

I shake my head. "I don't know what else to say," I tell her.

"Thank you for your time," she says. "Would you just pronounce and spell your name for the record, so we can be sure to get it right?"

"Jenni— Jen Brewer," I say. If I'm Jen at the diner, I guess I should be Jen on TV. "J-E-N B-R-E-W-E-R."

The light on the camera blinks off. The reporter slides down from her stool, and in the same move slides a business card across the counter. "If there's anything you'd like to add, feel free to contact me."

I clear her untouched cup of coffee as the cameraman leads the way out the door.

When I go to warm his coffee again, Cliff says, "You really saw it?"

I nod.

He covers my hand. "I'm sorry."

"Do you think it was wrong?" I blurt. "To talk to them."

"Wrong was what happened to Tariq," Cliff says. "You just gotta do what you gotta do."

KIMBERLY

I can't believe I kissed the Reverend Alabaster Sloan. I watch him on TV again, incredulous.

It was reckless and impulsive. Two things that I definitely am not. I am neat and organized, every hair in place. I mean, it's my job to be like that.

It must have flustered him, because he left his briefcase behind when he went out to the vigil. It was leaning against the stool in the room where I did his makeup, but after his remarks, he never came back inside. I guess the crowds rushed him away. I have it now, and I need to figure a way to get it back to him. Hopefully without making a fool of myself again.

We always have the TV on in the salon. We sit in the styling chairs and watch it when business is slow, which isn't really that often. But I can see it even when I'm working. Mostly we watch talk shows and fashion news, lighthearted things that people find relaxing. But lately no one can turn away from the news about Tariq.

It's not like anything new has happened. They just keep bringing on more experts to talk about different aspects of the case. A sociologist who explains the way gangs work. A legal scholar who explains why Jack Franklin hasn't been arrested and why he might not ever be. Another lawyer opposite him argues for why Franklin should be held accountable. Journalists scream about the racial injustice, as if it's new and unfamiliar. A problem that can be solved overnight, all because of Tariq.

It's fascinating, maddening, a train wreck you can't pull your eyes away from, however morbid. They announce that Reverend Sloan plans to stick around town until after Tariq's funeral. Plenty of time to figure out how to return the briefcase.

I can't believe I kissed him.

"I'm here to provide what comfort I can to Tariq's family and his community," Sloan says. They're replaying footage from last night. Flashbulbs going off in his face during the interview cast his skin in various shadows. He seems to glow, but no more so on television than he did up close. "And I'm here because this type of incident deserves national attention. We need to look hard at our laws, and at the prejudice in our own hearts, so that what happened to Tariq Johnson never happens to anyone else again."

My lips touched those lips. Mind-blowing.

TINA

It is not very good
When lots of things change all at once.

Things that can never happen now:
    Hear Tariq's voice through the wall
    Go to Rocky's store again
    See Mommy smile
    Walk down Peach Street and not feel like crying
    Eat Snickers anymore

7. MONSTERS

TYRELL

My skin is slick, the room pitch-black, but my eyes are open. All this old stuff floats at me out of the darkness.

When we were seven, the leader of the Kings was a guy called Sciss. As in scissors, I think. Sciss was a big guy, bigger than Brick, even. Or maybe he just seemed it because we were small.

Usually they left kids like us alone, which was fine because Sciss was pretty scary. On the day I'm thinking of now, we were more or less minding our own business too. Well, at least as much as we were minding everyone else's. Walking down the street, you can't help but notice things that are happening. We were strolling, me and Junior and Sammy and T—we were heading down Peach, in fact—when Sciss and some of his guys came bursting out of a building and running up toward us.

T grabbed my arm and Junior's. I took hold of Sammy, and we collided into each other, a small knot, afraid. But the Kings blew right by us, straight into the street. Their wind whipped around us, cold as the blades that glistened in their hands. They streaked between the parked cars, over the asphalt, and took hold of some guy getting out of his car.

They started beating him. A storm that swirled and pounded.

Someone help him, I thought. Through the flailing fists and legs, I could see the man, struggling and small. Bleeding. *Someone help him.*

But there was no one else around anymore. Just the Kings and the man and the four of us, frozen.

Sciss came toward us. Fast as a flash. No time to think, let alone flee. "Get along, now," he said. "You didn't see nothing."

"We didn't see nothing," Tariq repeated, the rest of us clustered behind him.

My eyes fell to the knife in Sciss's hand. The blade long and jagged in a hilt of red and black and steel.

"You like that?" He held it up, close to me. "You want a knife like mine? Maybe someday."

The only thing not trembling was the earth beneath my feet. Sciss laid his knife along the side of my face.

"You know what happens to snitches, don't you?" he said.

We nodded as sirens started up in the background.

Sciss growled at us. "Go!"

We ran.

"To the clubhouse," Tariq called as we dashed toward safety.

Our clubhouse was a tiny clearing inside the circle of bushes behind the gazebo in the community garden. It started out being the gazebo itself, but that only lasted as long as the day we decided on it. There was almost always some old lady with a sack of bread crumbs sitting in there, feeding a flock of disgusting-ass pigeons.

We hunkered down in the clearing, sitting cross-legged, knees to knees. Sammy was crying, but we all pretended he wasn't. We didn't even talk about it. We just put our hands in the dirt in front of us so our fingers overlapped like box flaps and made a pact.

"We won't be like them," Tariq said. "Let's never join." There was no discussion of any other gang. We lived in Kings territory.

"All for one and one for all," Sammy sniffled. We had just watched the movie of *The Three Musketeers*.

"All for one," I said.

"One for all," Junior added.

Then Tariq went, "One . . . two . . . three."

"I swear," we chorused.

It's one of those huge moments in my memory, when for a little while, we became all-powerful. We'd stared down certain death at the hands of Sciss and the Kings and proved we could survive. For a while it was like we were invincible as long as we stuck together. I don't think I've ever felt bigger than I did in that instant. I've gotten smaller and smaller ever since.

TINA

It's scary to go to sleep now.
The sounds in my room are the same.
The look of the dark is the same,
And the glow of my Smurfette nightlight.
But if there are monsters under the bed,
I won't know about it.
I won't be safe.
Tariq cast a magic spell to keep them out.
I don't know how long it will last,
Now that he's gone.

KIMBERLY

My shoes shush along the hotel carpet, on the seventh floor. I'd meant to leave the briefcase at the front desk, but when they called Reverend Sloan's room, he asked for me to be sent on up. My palms sweat against the leather handle of the case he left at the vigil.

This is uncharted territory. I'm not even sure how loud to knock. I raise my fist and rap the wood gently with my knuckles.

He opens the door. The room is dark, apart from a slit of light from the bathroom, and one from the bedroom. He flips a switch on the wall, brightening the foyer with overhead light.

He is still beautiful.

I hold out the briefcase. He takes it.

"Thank you. I appreciate your taking good care of it. I usually have staff that manages my things."

"You're welcome." I push down my embarrassment and offer him a small smile. My foolishness overwhelms me. Shocking, the things you do when you're sure you'll never see someone again. I seized what I thought was a fleeting moment, only to have it prolonged.

"Kimberly," Reverend Sloan says, "I'd like to talk to you about something." He holds the door open, and I walk into the center of his suite. The door closes behind us. We are alone. The room is calm and quiet, and Sloan looms large in the center.

Not once, all through school, was I ever called into the principal's office, but that's how it feels now.

There is a couch, an armchair, a coffee table, a dining table with chairs, a small kitchenette, and a desk. The bedroom is behind a whole separate door. It's the fanciest hotel room I've ever been in.

"My assistant had to remain in DC since this trip was so spontaneous," he says. "I could use some help while I'm in town."

"Help?"

"Managing my schedule. The makeup, like before," he says.

Exactly like before? I wonder, thinking about the kiss.

"I don't have any experience. Except for the makeup. I could also do your hair, if, you know . . ." *If you had any.* I let my voice trail off. *Stupid.*

He clears his throat, on a half laugh. "Trust me, you have the necessary skill set. It's a lot of holding my briefcase during interviews."

Inside I'm leaping and bounding and twirling. "Maybe," I hedge.

"It would be a paid position," he offers. I didn't think I could be bouncing any higher.

"I'd have to talk to Mollie," I tell him. My boss is pretty cool, but I don't know how she'd feel about me taking time off. Then again, she did send me to go make him up. "I don't know how much time I can get."

"She can call me if she wants to. I wouldn't need you full-time, and it'd just be a couple of days," he said. "But you seem quite capable."

"Thanks, Reverend Sloan."

"Al," he says. My face must look confused, because he clarifies. "My friends and colleagues call me Al."

I want to kiss him again, but I can't. I know I can't.

REVEREND ALABASTER SLOAN

It's flirting with danger, I realize. But I do need a hand. There's always a temp agency or consulting firm that can farm out someone, but it's hit or miss with temp hires, who typically don't really care. They're not always reliable. And there's no guaranteeing they'll be so pleasing to the eye.

"Come by in the morning, give me a touch-up," I tell Kimberly. "Then just go about your business tomorrow, talk to your boss, and we'll take it from there."

"Okay," she says.

"Tariq's funeral will be the following day. That's when I'll really need someone."

"Sure, that makes sense." She tips her face up. My gaze drops to her smooth throat, expanse of chest, deep cleavage I can see down into. She isn't dressed immodestly; she just has the kind of stunning figure that cannot easily be contained.

"Kimberly, thank you for coming by. And for the briefcase. I truly appreciate your diligence." I place my hand on her hip and steer her toward the door. So soft, so beautiful. She gazes up at me with admiring awe. It leaves me heady.

I'll be happy, having her around. Temptation keeps me on my toes.

God help me.

NOODLE

There's no parking close to the diner, so I idle in front of a hydrant and wait for Jennica to come out. When she does, she's moving slow, kind of dragging.

"Hi." We kiss. Then she moves to sit on her side of the car, instead of sliding up close to me like usual. I pull away from the curb. "What's wrong?"

She looks out the window. It's dark and late, but not that late. Hours to go before either of us has to be home.

Brick's place isn't far. Street parking's good; we land about a block away from his building. I kill the engine, lay my arm over the back of the bench seat. "You gonna tell me?"

"It was a rough day," she says. "These reporters came by."

"They bothering you?" I ask, wondering if I need to knock some skulls together.

"It wasn't that bad," she says.

Which was it, I wonder—rough or not bad?

"Here." I pop open the glove compartment. I've got a couple joints in there—literally tucked into a glove, which has saved my ass two times for sure when I've been pulled over and searched—and a flask. She reaches for the flask, which is unusual.

"I might be on the news," she says. "I guess we should watch later."

"Whatever you want," I answer. I'm starting to get pissed at this whole mess. Tariq goes down, and now the rest of us have to suffer.

"Are you mad?" she says.

I feel it rising in me. A fierce, churning ball in my gut. A building on fire. "Nah," I lie.

"It feels like you're mad at me."

"Why would you talk to reporters?" I ask.

"We're not supposed to. I know we're not supposed to." She pets my shoulder and my chest. Tries to kiss me. "I didn't talk about you. Maybe they won't even put me on."

Of course they will. Looking like she does, and talking good on top of it? Please. Of course they'll put her on. I'm going to have to watch it. I don't want to.

"Forget it," I say. "Talk to whoever you want."

"I want to talk to you."

"Well, I don't want to talk," I say.

"I'll make it up to you." Her hand slides across my thigh, inward. "I can do anything you want."

Her face is close to mine. And gorgeous, even through the pain in her expression. "Show me," I tell her.

She's very good with her hands, with her lips. She kisses me, works some kind of magic until the sense of frustration and sorrow rushes from me and she sinks into my arms. Over her head, I smoke.

We sit in the front seat for a while, watching the headlights of the passing traffic glide into a blur. I light another joint while

Jennica drains whatever's left in the flask. Until she's all soft and slumped against me.

"You feel better?" I ask her.

"Not really," she says.

"Let's go to Brick's," I say. He always has plenty more.

JENNICA

Noodle helps me out of the car, and I realize that whatever was in that flask was strong. It's hard to keep upright. My feet miss the curb. Noodle catches me with one strong arm around my waist. He might be thin and loose-looking, like his nickname, but every inch of him is muscled and sleek. I love how it feels when he scoops me close like this; there's no way to fall while he's holding me.

No point in looking for my balance, either. I spin into him, throw my arms around his neck.

"Dang," Noodle says. "You got fucked up fast."

The last time I ate was about a day ago. Which makes me stupid for drinking. And it probably hasn't even caught up with me all the way yet, which is bad, because when it does, we'll already be at Brick's and someone will put a drink in my hand and I'll forget that it's stupid to be drinking. Because I don't want to think.

Noodle laughs. "You're feeling good now, right?" he says.

Wrong. It just feels like I swallowed the fire that was burning all around me. Now it's inside me.

I shake my head against his neck. "Let's not go to Brick's."

"I already told him we were on the way," Noodle says. "Come on." He leads me along the sidewalk. Putting one foot in front of the other seems like a lot to manage.

In a more perfect world, I could just say no and go home. But the world grows less and less perfect by the minute. I know I can't make it on my own.

Noodle keeps his arm around me, firm and tight and safe. I lean against his shoulder and let the lights turn fuzzy in front of my eyes.

"Don't cry," Noodle says. "We're gonna have fun."

BRICK

"Whatta you make of this mess?" Noodle says. He looks across the coffee table at me. He's on the couch, and I'm in my chair—high-backed red leather with wings like a fucking throne. No matter how wild the party gets, no one sits in this chair but me. That's respect. I earned this position.

I got all the windows open to let in the night breeze, but it's still hot as a mother up in here. It's okay, though. My party's where it's at. Always. Can't do no wrong, can't get too hot. Music's pumping. The honeys dancing and sweating—that glisten on their skin, all sexy—usually I'm content enough to sit here, watching them move.

Tonight I can't get my mind off the shooting. Whenever a King goes down, it shakes up the world a bit, but it being Tariq this time cuts a deeper kind of way. He might've been dragging his feet on stepping into the Kings, but hell, he was already a brother.

"I said, whatta you make of this mess?" Noodle repeats. I heard him the first time.

By "mess," I imagine he means the vigil. Even more people showed up tonight than last night. Through the window screens, from eight floors up and a couple blocks away, under the jam that's playing, you can still hear the sounds of singing. Some low, sad thing that's meant to conjure angels out of the concrete. How long you got to walk these streets before you know? Ain't no angels coming.

"Tariq liked to screw with us while he was alive, and now he's doing it dead," I answer.

Noodle laughs. "It's a fucking circus."

"Even Sloan's here now. The story's not going away." I put my foot on the coffee table. Over Noodle's shoulder, the girls bob and swerve their hips. Off-the-hook sexy.

"It shouldn't have gone down like that," Noodle says. "Maybe they've got a point."

"We should get into it," I tell him. "Let people know that Franklin up and shot T for no reason."

Noodle looks confused. "Now you think T didn't have a gun?"

"Naw, I gotta figure out the gun, but that's just between us. Ain't you been watching the news?"

Noodle shakes his head.

"What matters is why Franklin got out of the damn car. Why'd he come running up on us in the first place?"

"I don't know," Noodle says. "He had some crazy in his eyes, that's for sure."

"I hear that. Listen, we need to set the record straight on this. That cracker was in the wrong, and we all know it."

"Sure." Noodle sounds a little wary.

"If it was the Stingers that came for T, it'd be over. We'd find them and take them out, if they weren't already locked up."

"You want to get revenge on Franklin?"

"They arrested his ass. And let him go. That ain't right." If the Stingers did the shooting, or us, someone would be halfway to the state pen by now. "We gotta let people know it ain't right."

"So say whatever you want." Noodle shrugs. "There's reporters all over the 'hood right now."

There's the rub. "Naw, I can't. You're gonna have to do it." No way I can admit I was at the murder scene and left. The cops already think they got a few things on me. They're just waiting for the other shoe to drop.

"What?"

"They already know you was there. You backed up Jennica's statement that T was unarmed—it's bullshit, but it's the better narrative."

"Narrative?" Noodle echoes. I grit my teeth. I'm losing him. Between the weed he's smoking and the weeds that just live in his idiot head . . . I don't know if he can even do what I'm asking.

"Story. Letting Franklin walk is bullshit. He's a murderer. T ain't deserve to go down like that, gun or no gun. You tell it to the reporters. Make sure they know."

"What good would it do?" he says. "We call attention to ourselves, we get more trouble."

"No press is bad press."

"Huh?" Noodle says.

"I saw that somewhere."

He nods, but I can see he ain't getting it. He might be my number two, but he's not the one I wanted.

"Hey, we'll talk about it tomorrow," I tell him. "Don't even worry."

Noodle's girl, Jennica, lies with her head in his lap, wasted drunk. She's usually better company. Everything with Tariq is just messing with her head. I get that. But I wish she wasn't out of it. She'd feel me. Maybe even have an idea about it. She's the right kind of smart.

Me, I've got any number of girls. In my phone, favorites four through eight and twelve through fifteen. Call 'em up, and any one of them will come running. That's how I like to play it. But I'm still looking for one I want to keep around. I glance down at Jennica again.

"I woulda cut Franklin," I tell Noodle, "if I knew he was gonna fire on T."

"What?" Noodle says, voice all fog. He tilts his head toward me.

"He was right next to me." The things I could've done rise up around me like smoke from Noodle's joint. He's so high now, he's barely with me. He won't remember what I'm saying. So I just say it, plain out loud.

"I feel bad," I say. "Franklin was right next to me. I coulda cut him. I coulda saved Tariq."

"Fuck, bro," Noodle says. "Tariq had it coming." He draws deep on the joint and sinks lower into the couch.

I hate him for a minute, hate both of them, for taking the easy way out, leaving me to sit in the smoke, watching Tariq fall over and over before my eyes, while I do nothing.

I sip a beer, but I know I got to keep my head on straight. Someone's got to be in charge.

WILL (AKA eMZee)

It's dark when I slip out the rec room window. I catch the mid-night bus from Steve's ritzy part of town over to Underhill. The other people on the bus are mostly workers on their way home. I recognize some of them. We nod. It's like a routine.

I wear the borrowed hoodie, but I won't cover my head unless I start a mural and I want to hide my face. It's necessary then. I'll try not to worry about it. I'm not going to do anything stupid and get myself shot like Tariq.

I like to mural, but I don't usually have the time or want to take the risk of it. It's not always that easy to find a big space when no one's looking. I got several murals up, but most of them have been tagged by other people, which is whack. I tag, but I don't tag other people's art. It's just disrespectful.

I tag walls and windows, mailboxes, manhole covers, side-walks, doors, poles—anything that doesn't move, plus buses and boxcars, which do. You ask anyone in Underhill whose tag is hot-test. They'll know.

My scrawl is up all over this town—the curls behind an *M* sharp like mountains with a *Z* cut like a lightning bolt. I once overheard someone saying it's the most recognizable tag to come along in a decade. Every night I'm out spraying. I own these walls. I own this 'hood.

I've never been caught. Not so much as a petty vandalism rap against my name. I've had to run a couple times, but I'm light and fast. I always get away. No one knows who I am, but everyone knows me. I like that.

It's my way of putting my stamp on the neighborhood.

This is where I'm from, and I miss it. These streets are still a part of me. I don't want Underhill to forget me.

8. LOCKED DOOR

EDWIN "ROCKY" FRY

Six A.M., I pull in the papers, like always. Today I'm dreading it. The news hasn't passed, it has only heated up.

FRANKLIN'S RELEASE STIRS CONTROVERSY; CITIZENS PROTEST

The cover image in the local paper is a crowd of people with hand-lettered signs camped outside the police station where Franklin was brought and released hours later. *"What kind of message does it send to the people of Underhill, when one of their own can be taken down with no consequences to the shooter?"* *one protestor wondered.*

MOM: "TARIQ DESERVES JUSTICE" — SLAIN TEEN'S FAMILY PROTESTS ALLEGED SHOOTER'S RELEASE

The national news printed his mother's full statement decrying the violence that took her son's life, and demanding justice. In the same article, Reverend Sloan calls for further investigation and suggests race bias. There's something to that. I remember how those police were in here, acting like they already knew what had happened, waiting for me to come around and agree.

POLICE CHIEF: "SELF-DEFENSE A PROTECTED RIGHT"

"We have no grounds on which to hold Mr. Franklin," said a police department spokesman in a statement. "The right to self-defense is protected under local and federal law. The tragic loss of one so young to violence renews our resolve to quell gang activity in Underhill."

Their "resolve" is evident as I glance out the front window. Cruisers have been rolling by with more frequency in the last seventy-two hours than ever before.

MELODY

For a Sunday morning, there's a heck of a lot of cops milling about Underhill. Tariq's shooting made them want to "crack down" on the neighborhood, my dad said. He was going on and on about it last night. "Why doesn't anybody crack down on the shooter, huh? Maybe those cops all secretly want to be like Jack Franklin."

People will talk, but I figure not much has really changed. There's always been cops hanging around, looking askance at everyone. I mean, that's just how it is.

Anyway, I'm not doing nothing wrong, so I go on past them and try to act like it doesn't matter. I'm on my way to Starwood House, the assisted living residence where I volunteer. It's not technically in Underhill, but it's close enough to walk if the weather is good.

Starwood's a big old place, all decked out to look like a mansion. I can't even guess how much it costs to live here, but it must be a lot. It's real fancy inside. They got a buddy program for some of the younger residents. I want to be a nurse practitioner, so I figure it's a good gig to warm up on.

I jog up the stone steps and wave to the security guard/ receptionist as I skip in the door. I poke through the rooms looking for Sheila, the developmentally delayed girl I usually play with. She's fifteen, but seems a lot younger. We're a good buddy match, because she likes to listen and I like to talk. Her brother pays for her to be here, they told me, on account of her needing full-time care. She's smarter than people think—she goes to school and everything—but she's not very physically coordinated, so she needs a lot of help with basic things.

I find her scream-crying in the corner of her room, huddled in a ball, with an activities staffer sitting on the end of the bed watching her. Sheila's typically very happy. Unflappably so.

My heart starts pounding extra hard. "What happened?"

"Someone told her about Tariq Johnson," the staffer tells me. "We can't calm her down."

"Did she know him?" I ask, although I suppose even the idea of what happened might be enough to set a person off.

"Their brothers are friends, or something."

That's not quite right, I'm sure. "Tariq didn't have a brother."

The staffer shrugs. "I don't know. That's all we could get out of her."

"Oh." Sheila's constant wail is alarming, like a siren screaming through town toward an unknown disaster. Makes me shiver, remembering the real sirens for Tariq a few days ago.

"You can take the day off, if you like. Obviously she's not in the mood to play."

"That's okay." I swallow. Volunteering's like a job to me. I never miss a week. What kind of nurse am I gonna be if I can't hang in there, right?

I go sit on the floor by Sheila. She leans her head on my shoulder. Snot-tastic.

"I cried when I found out, too," I tell her.

TINA

There is a way to open a locked door
You just get the key
From where Mommy keeps it hidden
On the hook inside the front hall closet
Stand on tiptoe
No big deal
Go right on down the hall
Turn the knob
Go inside
Tariq's room is the same
Smells like Tariq
(Kinda funky)
All Tariq's things
(A whole big mess on the floor)
I sit on the bed
The room is full of stuff
Why does it feel so empty?
Tariq's room is the same
But not the same
Without him.

TYRELL

Nothing is as simple as it used to be. We had such good times, the four of us. Running and playing and laughing, certain that the bad things in the world would never touch us. Not like life was perfect; Tariq's dad would disappear for months and years at a time, and Sammy never had a dad to begin with, and for a while Junior's family was so poor we had to sneak him food out of our lunch boxes. But it was all so normal. It was just part of us.

The first time we had a sleepover, it was at Sammy's house. Junior didn't have a sleeping bag, I remember, and so he almost didn't come, and then we had to go and get him because no way would we have as much fun without him, especially if we knew he was just sitting at home alone.

Between the four of us, we had three sleeping bags. So we unzipped them all and opened them up, then zipped them together into one super-huge bag big enough for the four of us. We all got inside, first Junior, then me, then T, and then Sammy. Four peas in a pod, so to speak.

It turned out Sammy sleeps like a tornado. Arms and legs all over the place. So he ended up with about half the bag, and me, Junior, and Tariq all piled up in the other half. After that night, we learned to let Sammy keep his own bag and to zip the other two together for the rest of us.

Sammy was the first to ditch us for the Kings, in the end. Too restless.

I don't know when or how the rest of us stopped sharing one bag. We kept sleeping over, and it kept being fun. We would stay up half the night goofing. Maybe it just got weird, you know, three guys in a bag.

But those sleepovers were maybe the best times we ever had—safe and close. Nothing outside could touch us.

JUNIOR

Tariq and I were best friends in second grade. It was just the two of us that year; we were the only ones of our friends together in the same class. We sat next to each other all the time.

We used to share our fruit at lunch. When you went through the line, after you got the hot meal, there would be a pile of fruit, and you could take one apple or one banana. Sometimes it was a pear or a peach or something like that, but usually it was an apple or a banana, and you had to choose. But we each liked both. So T would get the banana, and I would get the apple, and we would split them.

When I oathed in with the Kings and Brick gave me my knife, I showed it to T right away. He was disappointed, I think. First Sammy, then me walking out on our pact. It was kid stuff, but T and Ty took it real serious.

T didn't give me a hard time about it, though. He held my knife, in its sheath of red leather. Even made a joke out of it. "Damn, I guess I gotta join the Stingers now," he said. "Get me a yellow one, and we'll share." We laughed, and I felt like from that moment on, I had T's blessing to go on and do what I had to.

I still think about that now, eating off the metal trays in the prison cafeteria. Sometimes there is an apple or a banana, and when there is, I always think about him.

MS. ROSALITA

It is tempting to retreat to my small, private apartment. Fold myself into a book, or just appreciate the silence. But I head outside anyway. There is so much to enjoy in the world; how foolish to waste even an hour of it hiding away in avoidance of pain.

I take my place in the row of chairs along the fence outside the garden. The woven canvas straps are molded in my shape. I settle into place, and the fabric sighs as if it was expecting me. Small comforts are all I can rely upon today.

There was a time, years ago, when each passing hour held no meaning. There would be another, and another after that. A day felt like a lengthy endeavor; a year, unfathomably long.

I am no longer grasping great handfuls of time. A year seems long again now, not because so many stretch before me, but so few.

Redeema comes down the block toward me. She steadies herself with the cane she uses occasionally. I find myself smiling. It's funny; I still so often think of her as a girl, but today she looks like an old lady to me. We have become elders together, and yet I remember when she was born.

I was, for many years, the one the women turned to. I held her mother's hand through the pains and the pushing, helped to ease her troubled breaths. Redeema's was one of a thousand beautiful brown faces I was the first to lay eyes upon. I have a thousand children, though I never carried one of my own.

"Hello, Ms. Rosalita," she says, and I hear the voice of a child. She settles alongside me, hooking her cane on the chair arm. It's just the two of us for now.

"Looks like rain," I tell her, in an effort to keep things normal. The sky is cloudless, but gray.

"It is already raining," she answers.

I suppose. We rest in silence for a while, thoughts caught in each of our imperfect minds.

The pain is great today. As is the beauty and the joy. The young people who pass by wave to us. The smallest ones greet us with kisses and show-and-tell. *I got an A, Ms. Rosalita. . . . Hey, Mrs. J, look what I made.* They are excited, undamaged. They are our joy. We pat their cheeks and view their treasures with pride.

They spin away, always away. Too fast to understand, sometimes. They rush on, but we remain. They will come back, and we will be still here, as they expect us to be. We are the guardians.

In between each small flurry, we rest. We breathe. Redeema raises her face to the sky. "My children," she murmurs, and the sound of it aches.

I am expected to be wise. But it gets no easier, with time, to speak about a tragedy. We sit. After a long quiet moment, she puts out her hand. A very small move, little but a slight shift of fingers along the white plastic arm of the beach chair. My own fingers walk and bridge the gap to cup hers. We sit.

SAMMY

I polish up my piece real nice, in honor of Tariq. When I'm alone, I take it out and hold it in my hand, just feeling the weight of it. Thinking about next time I'm looking down someone else's barrel. Practice slipping it in and out of my belt.

I wanted a piece, because the best way to get made and move up in the organization is to ice someone. An enemy. As a show of loyalty. Prove how far you're willing to go. Jack Franklin woulda been a prime target. I'm never gonna miss an opportunity like that again.

Over at Brick's place in the afternoon, there's a bunch of us just chilling. It's mostly higher-ups, I realize after a while. Getting some business done. Brick never used to have this kind of time for me. I guess you can luck your way into moving up the chain, too.

I smoke a little J when someone lights up and hands it around. Just a sip.

"Yo, Sammy. Let me holla at you a minute," Brick says. He motions me over with a flick of his fingers.

I follow him into the bedroom. He closes the door behind us. Just me and Brick. We've never been alone like this before. He has a secret layer of drawers behind his closet that he opens with a clicker like a garage door. Hidden right in the wall. The drawers slide out. Smooth row after smooth row of knives and guns. A top-shelf arsenal.

"Whoa."

Brick grins. "Yeah."

I move closer to peer at the collection. I don't know much yet about different kinds of weapons, but it's a bit like looking at an expensive car. You can just tell it's high-end. Somehow.

"Why don't you show me what you're carrying." Brick's low voice, its too-casual tone, starts my heart pounding.

"What?"

He doesn't speak again. He knows I heard. I lift my shirt. Brick ignores the red-sheathed knife holstered at my waist. His eye goes to my opposite hip. Where the gun is tucked.

"That's a decent piece. Where'd you get it?" Brick asks me.

"I paid a guy for it." This piece is mine, fair and square.

"What guy?"

I grin. "Why? You need a referral?" One glance around at his arsenal says that's not likely.

"I'm trying to figure . . . ," Brick murmurs. He moves his hands out flat in front of him. Like he's running a turntable or moving puzzle pieces around on a table. "Based on where everybody was . . ."

He has a glinting look in his eye. I swallow.

". . . who coulda picked up T's gun."

"T didn't have a gun," I say.

"It was a smart move," Brick continues. "Whoever done it, I'd like to thank him."

His posture isn't thankful. I can only repeat it: "T didn't have a gun."

"That's what you tell other people," Brick says. "This is between us."

"What do you want me to say? You wanna meet the guy I bought it off last week? I'll take you over there. Anytime."

"I want you to tell me the truth."

I shake my head, having nothing to add. "All I saw was Jack Franklin. All I did was run." I'm not going to tell him how I thought about firing. I'm not going to put myself on the spot for having failed. It's hard enough in my own head.

Brick shifts toward me, real subtle. "I think you seen T with a gun. You seen him drop it when he got bit. You was closest. While we was all distracted by Franklin. . . . Tell me, Sammy, am I looking at that gun right now?"

"T didn't have a gun," I stammer. Then I realize I'm still holding up my shirt. I let it drop.

"You'd lie to protect him, wouldn't you?" Brick says.

I look him straight in the eye. "Yeah, I would," I answer. "But not to you."

BRICK

"He got out of the car and fucking shot T," I tell Noodle. "That ain't self-defense."

"Stingers cut our guys down for less."

"It's different," I say. *Because it's Tariq*, I want to add. But I don't. Him and Noodle never got along.

"No, it ain't."

But it is. If the Kings are about anything, it's standing up for your brothers.

Noodle's right, we've lost plenty of other brothers. Why's it so much harder than usual to imagine life without T? I don't understand this need to re-sculpt the world in my mind.

Maybe it's just the history. Maybe I'd feel this way about any of the guys closer to me. Or maybe T felt more like an actual brother, because of our sisters.

We used to walk Sheila and Tina down to Roosevelt Park in the afternoons together. You get to know a guy in a different kind of way, sitting on a park bench side by side, watching little girls play.

You gotta chat about something or be bored out of your skin, so we pretty much talked about everything. The side of me that my sister knows is different from what other people know. You got to be more open around kids like them. I think T was the same. So we got deep, and pretty easy. That softness we hide striding down the street—how do you hide it when you got to bandage up a skinned knee and kiss it to make it better?

They liked it when we would push them on the swings and sing silly songs at them. In front of another dude, that shit's just embarrassing. But if you gotta do it, you might as well own it, right? We did friggin' harmony.

One day, I remember, we were sitting on the park bench when all these cops rolled up. We witnessed a bust of King dealers at the other edge of the park.

T laughed. "Weren't we saying just the other day that they were prime for a bust?"

"Yeah, they got no organization," I agreed. "You can see the exchange from a mile away. Do they think they're subtle?"

"That's a management problem," T said. "They're just being stupid."

"Someday I'm gonna run that joint."

T laughed. "Yeah, right."

"I could do it better."

"Well, duh."

I grinned. "You can be my backup."

"Oh, sure," he said. "Just one problem. I'm never joining up with that. I got other plans."

That was how it started. We came up with a whole new strategy for the organization those afternoons. I was already doing some low-level running. It wasn't out of the question that I was gonna move up. And soon enough, T stopped saying "never" and started saying "if." And soon enough after that, "when."

NOODLE

I gotta be honest. Ask me three days ago, I'd have said I wanted that little fucker gone. Now I gotta go out front and talk to people? Just like I told Jennica not to.

I'm so steamed over it, it's hard to even tell her.

"I hated that punk." I pound the steering wheel, driving her to work. "Damn it. Why couldn't he just die normal?"

"Or not at all," Jennica says softly.

"Brick's making a mistake," I tell her. "We oughta let well enough alone."

"It's not a bad thing to stand up for someone."

"He wants me to get up there and lie. *Tariq was innocent. Tariq was unarmed.* What the hell is that?"

"You think he had a gun?" she says.

"How come you didn't see it? I don't know where you could have been looking."

She stares out the window.

"Asshole punk," I mutter.

"You shouldn't speak ill of the dead," Jennica says. "It's bad luck."

As if my luck can get any worse. I thought things were looking up for me when Tariq went down. Now it just seems like he's bound and determined to bring me down with him.

JENNICA

It's not like we were friends. That's what I keep thinking. I gotta snap outta this. I feel heavy, like I'm walking through water, or waist-high sand.

I wipe down the tables. My head still aches from yesterday.

Noodle comes back early, an hour before the end of my shift. Says he's checking up on me, but he's still all on edge. I bring him pie and coffee. Got to be on the house, but if Cory is watching, I'll end up having to put it in out of my tips. I set the plate down.

Noodle picks up my fingers. "Hi."

"Hi."

"You okay?"

Nothing is okay. When I close my eyes, even to blink, I see pools of red and white, like a blur that never goes away.

"I'm fine. Just tired."

"Babe," he says, "you're acting weird."

"We saw someone shot," I remind him. "It's not like business as usual."

Noodle raises a shoulder. "Tariq had it coming," he mutters. "It is what it is."

I want to crack his smirk. Tariq died right in front of us. Noodle may not have liked him much, but doesn't he care at all?

NOODLE

Jennica's not herself anymore. Ever since Tariq. I try to tell her it's part of the life, but she gets this closed-up look on her face, so I figure it's best not to say anything. We can just get high and try to forget about it. That's part of the life too.

She finishes her shift and gets her purse from the back room.

On the sidewalk, before we get to the car, I take her shoulders in my hands. I know now what it is I'm seeing in her eyes—a thing I've forgotten. Because I don't let myself feel that way anymore.

"It scared you, right?"

"Of course it scared me," she says. "You weren't scared?"

"I ain't scared of nothing."

"Not even dying? Or being shot?" she whispers. "Everything just ending?"

"Naw." I shrug. Maybe it's in me somewhere, but I ain't gonna try and look for it. I buried it good and deep. Back in juvie, with some big King telling me to kneel or get cut. Back home, when Pop used to scream about something or other. Down on the street, when guys got cut down in front of me. The first time I held a knife, or a piece. The first time I used one. It all piles on top and the fear gets pushed down; it isn't so big now. I know I'm going back inside someday. I know I'm gonna get cut down someday, too. It's the life, though. It's just how it is. I ain't scared of it, I'm just living it.

"You ain't got to be scared," I tell Jennica. "I'm here to look out for you."

With my arm across her shoulders, she seems small. Not like when I look at her across a room.

"Can you take me home?" she says.

"Naw. Brick's waiting. We're gonna go for a drive."

"I don't want to ride along anymore."

"Aw, come on, sugar." I kiss her. "You know I like you with me."

"I don't want to go tonight." She shrugs away. "I don't want to be out there with them, after the other day."

I put her in front of me again. "Hey. It's going to be okay. I promise."

Her eyes fill with tears. "How can you say that so easy?"

"Don't be upset." I hate it when she cries.

"I'm not a fucking light switch," she snaps. "It upsets me. I'd have to be a pretty cold bitch for it not to."

I hate it more when she's angry. Is that a roundabout way of calling me cold?

"Why you so hung up on Tariq?" I say. "He was a stupid prick, like I been telling you. You got a thing for him? You got something you want to say to me?" I put out my arms.

"Oh, for God's sake." She swipes at her lash line, sweeps away the dam of tears.

"Answer me." I wrap my hand up in her hair, hold her head back.

"Ow."

"Answer me!"

"Fuck, stop it," she cries. The tears are real now. Flowing. "Let me go."

"Don't forget where you belong," I whisper. "Tariq was nothing. Say it."

"Tariq was nothing," she whispers. "I belong with you."

TYRELL

Good memories of Tariq come easy sometimes. Those thoughts get me through the day, going to school and back, past the block spilling over with vigil flowers, past Rocky's store, past the steps of the church where tomorrow I have to go in and see T in a coffin.

The good memories are hard enough to carry, because they remind me: T won't be smiling anymore.

We won't be laughing together anymore.

We won't be hanging together anymore.

T and I were friends forever. A lot of history. A lot of good times, and in our case, just as many bad times. Those memories come in the middle of the night, when I'm trying to sleep.

I sit on the kitchen floor, feeling the hum of the refrigerator on my back, and eat six vanilla puddings, sucking them straight out of the containers, scraping the opaque plastic with my fingers to get every last drop.

Then I eat the snack-size bags of chips: Doritos, Fritos, Baked Lay's.

Then the string cheese.

My mom packs this food in brown bags for my dad to take to work for lunch. He'll be angry tomorrow, when there's nothing for him to eat. But it's okay. He's always angry with me.

Tariq knew why. He knew, because I told him. The things I never told anyone else.

T was the only one who knew the truth about how I broke my wrist in seventh grade.

The only one who knew why my dad really hates me.

The truth hits me hard, right along with the sugar rush.

There's no one alive who knows these things about me.

9. ASHES TO ASHES

TOM ARLEN

First thing when I wake up, I poke around online to catch the news. I do it quietly, still in my bedroom with the door shut. The rest of the house is a news-free zone.

Jack's not interested in the coverage. He's sure of what he saw, what he did.

I want to be so sure. Every time I get a chance, I sneak a peek. He's not awake yet, so I hustle downstairs and fetch the paper off the front porch.

I can't deny I'm hooked on the story. It's the closest I've ever come to having a foot in something important. It's fascinating to see the incident morph and fester.

The street is lined with news trucks. Local news, national news, all the major networks. Parked vans with big antennae mounted on top, stretching around the corner toward the church where the funeral will be held this afternoon.

Tariq Johnson will be buried today, but his death isn't over. I doubt it will feel over even tomorrow. Look at what's happening around town. A photo montage of angry protestors with placards outside police headquarters. Another crowd gathered on the steps of City Hall. They're even clustered outside Jack's house in one image, which backs up what he's been saying. Not that I ever doubted him.

But as I scroll through the pages, I suddenly feel less certain. When Underhill bands together like this, I should be a part of it. It's my neighborhood, and I've been here long enough to know that guys like Tariq Johnson don't always get a fair shake.

I don't think Jack was wrong, or I wouldn't have him in my house. But if I hadn't been there, if I hadn't seen, I'd surely be marching right along with them.

JENNICA

I enter the beauty salon wearing really big sunglasses, like one of those women on TV who's just been given a black eye by her husband. I guess I get it now, the urge to hide yourself after something strange and hurtful happens.

"Hi," says one of the stylists as I walk in the door. She's beautiful and large, and though she looks only vaguely familiar, for some reason, I want very badly to hug her. "What can I do for you?"

"Just a trim, and style."

"Have a seat." She lifts herself out of the chair where I'm to sit, where she was waiting for a customer, I guess. For me.

"Thanks." The TV is on, some talk show. I'm relieved. I don't want to see the same picture of Tariq. I'm stuck enough with the picture in my head.

"I'm Kimberly."

"Jennica."

"Nice to meet you." She combs my hair with quick, smooth strokes.

"Ow." My neck is still sore from where Noodle jerked my head last night.

"You okay?" Kimberly says.

"Yeah." I don't think Noodle knew he hurt me. I know he didn't mean to. He loves me.

Kimberly gets out the scissors and starts trimming my ends. Just the slightest bit. Swiftly. It looks good.

Usually my auntie cuts my hair at home. I can't remember the last time I was in a salon, if ever. Maybe when I was little. Auntie Anjelica does a pretty nice job, and my hair is good enough to not need much work. I always just wash it myself. So I can't help the tears that leak out as Kimberly lays me back in the neck cradle and massages my head under the gentle flow of water. It feels amazing.

I don't really have the money to pay for this haircut, even with my new hundred dollars. I really should use that for something more practical. New work shoes, some savings, or a little something extra to help my auntie with rent. I'm desperate, is all. I keep hoping something is going to lift me out of this feeling. That something will happen and I can start breathing again.

KIMBERLY

"I want to look good at Tariq's funeral," Jennica says as I'm washing her hair. "That's so weird, right?"

"It's not," I can honestly tell her. "A lot of people do that."

"Yeah?"

"Yeah. There's nothing wrong with dressing for an occasion. Even a sad one."

"I guess that makes me feel better," she says, in a voice that doesn't seem true to that.

"I knew Tariq too. He wasn't my favorite person." I don't know why I'm admitting this to her, of all people.

"I did CPR on him," she whispers. "It didn't work."

"You were there?"

"Uh-huh." Tears flow from her eyes, mingling with the spray of my shower hose.

"That's intense."

"I can't deal with it," she says. "I keep seeing it."

What do I do with that? "Just relax," I tell her. "Try to relax." I massage creamy shampoo into her hair.

"That feels good."

"You have really pretty hair."

"Thanks."

Over her head, I look at myself in the mirror. I wouldn't have gone to the funeral, but now I'll be there, helping out Reverend Sloan. Al.

I'll probably do my hair up nicely, too.

NOODLE

I don't know what you're supposed to wear to this kind of thing. Seems only right to show a bit of respect at a funeral, maybe a step up from what I would wear down the street.

I've got a dark suit. The one I wore when my Pops got bit, and when my cousin came home from Iraq messed up so bad they couldn't even open the casket.

I think about the dark suit, but no. I can't put that shit on. Not for Tariq.

It hangs at the back of my closet. All the way back, where I don't have to look at it. I don't want to think about the day it comes up useful again.

TINA

I am a big girl—
I can stay home alone.
No, Mommy says. *I want you close to me.*
Too many people now, when we go outside.
I know, Mommy says. *But it's just for a little while.*
"Let's give away all the other people," I say, "and get Tariq back."
It's a good idea, but it makes Mommy cry.

VERNESHA

If it wasn't happening to me, I would be all over this. Mom and I would be glued to the TV, waiting for the mother of the poor slain boy to emerge. What would she say? Would she cry? Would she rail against the wrongness, would she call out for blood, or would she rise to the level of forgiveness, plead for the mercy of God?

It's strange, thinking this. Like stepping outside myself.

My son wasn't perfect, but he was mine. The world isn't perfect, but he should still be in it.

I wish I could hate Jack Franklin. I know how it feels to hate—hatred would be more bearable than this sorrow. Anger would be more bearable than this sorrow.

If it wasn't happening to me, I'd be home, eating chips or something straight out of the bag and hating Jack Franklin. Relishing how much I hated him from afar, for putting out his hands and ending that poor black boy's life.

If it wasn't happening to me . . .

But it is. I have to remind myself. It *is* happening to me.

REVEREND ALABASTER SLOAN

The reporters shout questions. They swirl. A breeze like the devil around us.

"Vanessa! Vanessa!" they call out.

Vernesha's blank gaze is interrupted by a series of blinks. "Vernesha," she says automatically, as if she's been correcting people's pronunciation of her name all her life. She probably has. Cameras and mikes hover around us like flies. She stands stiffly, facing the flashes and the jostling cacophony.

They clamor. "Vernesha! Vernesha!"

Questions like popcorn. Her gaze like ice.

"Give her some space," I say, arcing my arm in front of her as a shield while we make our way to the church steps. Media vultures. She's going to speak. I just want to get her in position.

Vernesha reaches up and clutches my protective hand. Her small fingers fold around my thumb. They film it. A mother's desperate touch. I wonder what we will all think, seeing it on giant flat screens. Will it make people feel Tariq's death a little harder? Will it be the tug on their heartstrings that makes it all too much, that makes them turn to a convenient comedy to take their minds off the harsh corners of the world?

Black mesh microphones jam into our faces.

Vernesha leans into them. "Thank you for coming," she says. She releases my thumb, so I step back, far enough to give her space to speak, but not so far that I'm out of frame.

"It's becoming clear to me that Tariq's murder is no longer only a private tragedy for me and my family; it's a public one, and suddenly the whole world is watching our little corner of Underhill. I wish it hadn't taken my son's death to wake you to the reality of violence in black communities," she says. "I've been in this church plenty of times for other mothers' sons. They and I all wish you'd gotten here sooner."

I'm blown away. Inspired.

REDEEMA

Them Kings is here. Rows and rows of them. Them cameras too. Rows and rows of them.

Vernie walks with her back tall. Straight to the microphones.

"Thank you for coming," she says. She speaks good. My heavy heart rises; pride keeps it from falling right out my chest. The weight of all that sorrow.

Lord Jesus. My heart holds much too much today.

All the lights and the noise, a fierce sorta mess. Tina noses right against my skirts. Poor baby. I hold her close. I don't know how it is inside her mind, and there ain't no sense to make of this anyhow. I look up at the sky and will the hand of God: *Come down. Protect her.*

My daughter made it clear: My job today is Tina. Didn't say nothing, just pushed her precious baby into my arms. There's a job to do.

I've watched Vernie's babies from the time they were new, half raised them, but when it came to looking out for Tina, that job was always Tariq's, in a way. He took the role of big brother so serious. Tina loved that boy something powerful. I don't know if she'll ever understand why he's gone. Or if I will.

SAMMY

The coffin is closed by the time I get there. I'm glad about that. I had it in my head that it was gonna be open and I was going to have to see him.

Last time I saw T alive, I was showing him the ropes. I wanted him to be my bag man, holding the dope. It's the riskiest position in the hydrant roll, but everyone starts in that job.

I had to reassure him. He looked a little uneasy, until I told him, "Look, I pull a hundred bucks a night for a couple hours' work. Easy."

T grinned when I said that.

I smiled too. He was starting to get hooked on the idea. I could see it in his eyes.

"That's more than I thought," he said.

I put my arm around his shoulder. I was wearing my Kings jacket, unzipped, and one wing of it folded around him. "It'd be just like old times," I promised. "You wanna start tonight?"

"We'll see," he said. But he didn't walk away for a couple more minutes.

BRICK

Here comes Tyrell. Walking with his head down and sidestepping the crowds. I never understood what Tariq saw in that small fry. Tariq wasn't so big himself, physically, but his voice and his personality made him seem about as big as me. Tyrell, on the other hand, manages to seem smaller than he is. Folded up, or something.

To be truthful, I'm not sure if he has what it takes. Only reason I ever tried to hook Ty was that it seemed like him and Tariq were something of a package deal. *There's gonna come a point when you need brothers*, I'd tell him. T would throw his arm around Tyrell's shoulders. *I got brothers*, he'd say. *From way back.*

I knew he counted me as one of them. That's why I let it slide when he put me off. In the long run, the Kings had him. That much was clear. But Tariq woulda busted out any trick you can imagine to protect Ty.

My boy's going to college, he'd brag, even when Ty wasn't around and we could be real. Maybe so, I figure, but that's two years off. Till then, Ty's walking alone.

I've seen him the last couple of days, skulking around, flinching at his own farts. The Stingers razz him, my guys razz him, and he can't handle it.

Tariq managed it all so natural, so easy, that Ty's never had to face the real pressures of the street. He ain't equipped. Helping him out is the least I can do. All he needs is some red around his shoulders; after that, *all* the Kings will take care of him. He'll be one of our own.

It's what T would have wanted.

TYRELL

It's a hard enough day. I don't need another layer on it. Brick looms larger than ever.

"Ty," he says. I don't want to be nicknamed. Not by him.

I lash out. "What?"

Brick holds up a hand, all innocent. "Chill out. I was just going to say sorry, man."

"Oh." But it's hard to relax with him standing so close.

Brick puts a heavy arm across my shoulders and draws me to his side. It feels . . . strangely good. I don't want it to.

"Tough day," Noodle says. "For everyone."

"Yeah." I look at my shoes, polished up nice the way my grandpa used to insist for formal occasions. But he's gone too. And Tariq. All the big arms on my shoulders. Now there's only Brick.

"You know we're here for you," Brick says. "Whenever you're ready."

"Thanks." I straighten my shoulders, shrugging him off.

"We'll be by to check up on you," Noodle says. He says it real kind. Not even looking at me, just rubbing a smudge off the back of his hand. "You hear me?"

"I'm fine," I answer. Try to sound brave. Bigger than I felt underneath Brick's arm. "You don't have to do that."

"What are brothers for?" Brick says. My stomach goes down like an elevator. What would Tariq say? Something quippy.

169

Something quick. Something to let them know they can't claim me like that.

I can't think of a damn thing. I just stand there. Down the aisle, in front of the altar, is the casket, gleaming white. Little spikes of terror pierce me. Barbs of sadness right behind. Tariq will never say a thing again. I'm on my own now.

"You know where you're sitting?" Noodle asks.

"Up front," I say quickly. Before they invite me to the back rows, all red and black and full of 8-5 Kings.

Brick clamps a hand on my shoulder. His jacket fans open, and I can see the huge knife sheathed at his waist. "Catch you later, Ty."

They saunter away. I wipe at the little patches of skin in front of my ears. I'm sweating from under my hair.

I'm really good with problems. I can solve a differential equation in my head. I chew through trig angles like candy. I know this, and it just makes it worse. Because I don't know how to solve this one.

JENNICA

Noodle looks like the others, black jeans hanging low, covered by the tail of a white button-up shirt. Red jacket. Black tie, all funky and crooked.

I put my hands on his chest. "Oh, come on," I tell him. My fingers fumble to straighten his tie. He stands still over me, lifting his chin.

He won't apologize for last night, and I won't ask him to. We'll just go back to business as usual and pretend there isn't anything wrong. I guess we've done it before. I guess we've done it a lot, now I think about it.

We sit with the Kings contingent in the second-to-last row. Noodle rests his hand on my thigh, but he might as well be covering all of me. I'm protected, possessed. Untouchable.

It's not that I don't get it. The strength in numbers. How easy it is to sit and be surrounded by them. But I know enough to realize that the sick feeling in me is only going to grow, like a seed in the right soil.

I want out of this. I want out of what Noodle calls "the life." I want my own life. Away.

I don't want it to be this way forever, watching the guys I know die at one another's hands, the rest shrugging it off like it's just another weekday, just another shooting, just another death to swallow.

Reporters and cameras crowd the steps of the church. It was hard enough to get in; I can't imagine how it'll be to get out.

BRIAN TRELLIS

I have to cover my face just to get inside the church. Some of the TV people want to hail me as a local hero for standing up to Tariq Johnson; the rest want to throw questions at me, like they're trying to catch me in a lie.

I'm no hero. I can't think of a heroic thing I ever done in my life before that day. And obviously, now that doesn't count, either.

Tariq Johnson was clearly up to no good, one way or another. Rocky says he wasn't a thief, but he was . . . something. He was definitely one of the gang, the way they were ragging on him. So familiar. Like brothers.

He had a gun in his hand. I'm sure of it. I laid eyes on it. I mean, I must have. The deep-stabbing kind of fear I felt; that doesn't come from nowhere. Certainly not from a Snickers bar. I know I stared into the deep black hole in that glinting barrel.

My hand on his shoulder. He flinches. I relive the moment over and over.

The shots. *Pop.* Pause. *Pop.*

Here's where it all goes wrong, though.

Tariq falls, I turn. Jack Franklin's standing there. He lowers the gun, meets my eye for one split second. Nods. Then he takes off running.

I've seen that look often enough. It took me years to understand it. It's a white-man-to-white-man glance: *We're in this together.*

Franklin thought he was saving a fellow white man from the clutches of an 8-5 thug.

People make mistakes. They look at the surface of things and see what they want to. Jack Franklin looking at me. Both of us, looking at Tariq.

If I don't step in Tariq's way, Jack Franklin never gets out of the car. Guaranteed. However right, however wrong, Tariq Johnson got shot because of me. He's dead because of me.

KIMBERLY

The pastor's anteroom, behind the nave of the sanctuary, is both cool and stuffy. A strange mix of fresh-blown air and dusty old tapestry. Pastor Birch has been kind enough to allow Reverend Sloan to join him here, waiting for the service to begin.

"Excuse me." They glance up as I enter.

"Yes, Kimbee?" says Pastor Birch.

My face flushes, but hopefully they can't see it in the dim light. A childhood nickname doesn't exactly fit the image of me I want Al to see.

"Pastor, may I?" I wave my giant makeup pouch. Al surely needs a touch-up before going on camera again.

"Of course," he answers, motioning me inside.

"I'll just be a minute."

Al's attention goes to my figure, the way it does sometimes. It's flattering, and not at all creepy, the way it can be from other men when they check me out. I chose this dress especially for him, after trying on everything funeral-appropriate in my closet. The gray jersey hugs my hips. The fabric forms an X over my chest and my cleavage. His eye follows the line of my breasts, and lingers on the simple stone pendant resting against them. For the first time in a long time, I feel genuinely sexy.

I look at him through my lashes, unzipping the pouch. "Is there anything else you need, Reverend?" I feel like I shouldn't call him by his first name in this room, or in front of Pastor Birch.

"Thank you. I'm fine for now, Kimberly."

"Just a tiny bit," I decide, sweeping a sponge over his cheeks. "You're looking pretty good."

"Great."

His knee nudges between my thighs. Accident, I'm sure. I part my legs a bit, though. Move closer.

When I'm done, I lean back. Al raises his eyes from my chest. "Thanks."

"No problem. I'll be right in front, if there's anything else I can get for you."

Pastor Birch glances at me over half glasses as I slide toward the door.

TYRELL

I escape through the church halls toward the Sunday school class-rooms, heading for the men's room farthest from the entrance. The door pushes open with a familiar groan.

"Hi, Tyrell," someone says. I flinch at the sound of my own name. The conversation with Brick left me skittish.

It's Tariq's father. Of course he would be at the funeral.

He runs a paper towel over his face. "I didn't think anyone else would come back here."

Me either, to be honest. "Hi," I say. "Long time no see."

I don't know how Tariq himself would feel about his dad being here. The guy hasn't been around since maybe sometime in middle school. We don't talk about our dads that much.

"I've been away," he says. All the way across town, probably.

"Yeah." What else is there to say? "Well, I'm sorry," I add, shaking his hand.

"Yeah." He coughs some stuff out of his throat. "You guys still tight like you used to be?"

I nod.

He sits on the random folding chair that's set up behind the door. It wobbles under his weight. He's not that big a guy—it's just a crappy chair. It's probably been here a hundred years. I've never seen anyone actually use it.

It's weird, seeing him in a suit. It's doubly weird because I never realized how Tariq looks exactly like him. It's like looking at a future person that I'm never going to know.

"I remember one time, we all went to the zoo," he says. "You remember that? I took you boys. And some other kid."

"Junior, I think." It seems right to hedge, even though I remember exactly. "Junior Collins."

Tariq's dad snaps his fingers. "Right. Junior. Yeah. I remember now. You guys still tight, too?"

"Junior's locked up."

"That's too bad," Tariq's dad says. "You were always such good kids."

He says it as if he knows. As if he was there.

"You were such good kids," he murmurs. "Where did it go wrong?"

A thousand answers come to mind.

How about the day you showed Tariq your back?

It's Underhill. That's just how it goes.

We were good. It wasn't us that went wrong.

I have to bite the words back, and I barely manage. I came here to be alone, not to be nice.

But Tariq's dad is crying. Tears slipping out. I'm not sure he even notices. And I *am* nice.

So I lean against the bathroom wall and look away from him. I don't answer. It's the best I can do.

TINA

Coffin: white
Skin: brown
Flowers: red and yellow and orange and pink
People: sad
People: crying
People: talking and laughing and hugging
People: too many
People: too close
People: touching me
Under the pew: safe place to hide
Music: loud
People: wailing
People: talking to Jesus, asking Him why
Fingers: in my ears
Music: sweet
Coffin: lid closed
Skin: out of sight
Cousins: carrying coffin
Coffin: out of sight
Bye-bye
I don't want to really say it
Bye-bye
Mama: head down

Nana: holds my hand
Kings: *You ain't never got to worry. We take care of our own.*
Big board of photographs: still, so still
Tariq:

STEVE CONNERS

I'm admittedly curious about the Tariq Johnson funeral coverage. It's lunch hour, so I throw on sweats and power up the treadmill in my office suite. Flip on the news and start walking. Reverend Sloan headlines the press conference outside the church.

"Tariq Johnson's death is inexcusable," he's saying. His voice vibrates with intensity. "Too many have struggled for too long to allow the justice system to ignore race-based violence.

"What Jack Franklin thought he saw in his mind might have justified taking lethal action—but what he saw was not the way things were. He didn't take a second to think. This is action before thought, and he deserves to suffer the consequences.

"These allegations will not die just because the police have chosen to release Franklin from custody. These allegations will not die just because authorities do not know Franklin's current whereabouts. These allegations will be answered, and Jack Franklin must be held accountable."

I kick up the speed. Sloan speaks to the point well.

"The people of this community, the people of this nation, will not rest until Jack Franklin is brought to justice for taking the life of one of our sons. Yet another of our boys has perished by the gun. 'Live by the gun, die by the gun,' they say. Well, Tariq Johnson had chosen not to live by the gun. Despite enormous social pressures to join a gang, to become a part of the destructive street culture that is eating through the hearts of our young people."

The B-roll of the run-down section of Underhill where Johnson lived runs onscreen.

I haven't been to Underhill in so long. I can't put my finger on the last time. Maybe a few years ago, back when I would drive in to pick up Carla. But come to think of it, she usually just came to me.

From some things, it's easier to avert your eyes.

The footage of the church shows all manner of people coming and going. Leather-clad gang members, community leaders, young parents with small children in tow. The gang boys throw up signs and fists, looking tough and projecting a sense of power. There are all kinds of power—gang-type violent authority, sports-type physical prowess and social prestige, material wealth and economic dominance, power that comes from leadership, intellect, scholarship, knowledge. It's what you buy into, in a sense. The kind of power you seek depends on your worldview—what is necessary to survive, and what is most important.

When I was young, I knew I could be anything. My skin wasn't going to hold me back. Will doesn't have that feeling, and all I've been trying to do is instill it in him. Everything I am, everything I do, is not *because of* my race, nor *in spite of* it . . . it's regardless of it.

Will keeps saying, *I'm from there*, like it's something worth bragging about. I'm not a from-the-'hood black man. I can't understand the pride he feels about Underhill. The place is a dump. Look at it.

I punch up the speed. Time to really burn. The footage

continues, on an endless loop. Same faces. Same story. Same message. Same gut-tugging feeling that it's wrong, all wrong.

Sweat starts to pour from me. I pound the treads like I can somehow get ahead of it. I always get ahead. Except I can't fight the feeling that there's no running from this. No matter how far you get from a place like Underhill, it's all still right on your heels.

NOODLE

Brick says, "Now."

I step toward the cameras. My palms are sweating, and my eyes are tight. We practiced this. I'm no wordsmith, but I'm just gonna do my best. Brick's the boss, and here's my chance to show him I'm still the right number two.

Reporters throw questions at me like hand grenades. I'm right in the line of fire.

"We were just kicking it. All in fun," I answer.

"Wasn't there a fight going on?"

"That was between us. Jack Franklin wasn't no part of it. I don't know what he thought he was doing."

"But Tariq Johnson was armed."

All I want is to say *hell, yes.* But I can feel Brick watching me. It's impossible to be anything but what he asked me to be. "No reason to think that. Question is, why was Franklin running up on Tariq?"

"Did Tariq Johnson rob the convenience store? Was it some kind of initiation?"

I scoff. "Nobody steals from Rocky, man. He takes care of this 'hood. Nothing but respect."

"Johnson is also suspected of assaulting another man that afternoon—Brian Trellis?"

"Tariq was the one defending himself, man. That light-skinned brother ran up on him. He was minding his own business. We was chatting."

"Was there an argument?" The questions go around in a circle. I can barely see the faces for all the lights. But it gets to a place where I'm kinda having fun with it.

"Naw." I shrug. "Sometimes we get loud, but we were just having fun. People see guys like us having fun and being excited, and they think we're causing trouble. It's prejudice, man."

I'm on a roll. "Why'd Jack Franklin stop his car? Why'd he get out and run up on Tariq? Ain't no self-defense about it when you the one who walked into the situation."

"Was Tariq Johnson a member of your gang?"

My gang? I feel myself puff up a little. That's right. "It ain't illegal to be part of an organization," I say. "You think anyone wearing red around Underhill deserves to get shot?"

On and on. I'm into it now. With all this attention, I can almost forget I hated the little fucker. Tariq dead might be doing me some good after all.

"Listen—" I'm about to lay some more knowledge on them, when the mob of reporters suddenly surges to my right. They pivot away from me like one animal, amid shouts of "The family's coming out! There's the mother."

My eyes are a sea of fading bright spots. Brick steps up and slugs my arm. "Yeah," he says. "That's what I'm talking about."

TYRELL

It's some kind of slow-motion freak show. Reverend Sloan steps away from the mikes. The lights are bright and flashing, and I don't know why I'm still standing here, except that it's hard to believe what I'm seeing. The reporters grab for anything, like dogs after a bone. Barking just as loud. Right here on the steps of our own church.

The whole thing is surreal. Not just the fact that Tariq is gone, but the fact that the story is all over the news every night. This melee.

Noodle steps up to the mike. He starts talking about Tariq and how wrong it all is. Noodle wasn't exactly Tariq's biggest fan. Why's he up there talking about Tariq as "one of our own"? It's all lies. Except—I don't know. Maybe it isn't.

I read in the paper about how they found Tariq wearing a do-rag in 8-5 red. A week or so ago, Tariq was talking about the Kings again. He got like that from time to time. We all did. And I talked him down off it, because that was our deal. Did he go back on me?

There's no "all" anymore. We used to hold out, me and Sammy and Junior and T. Like the four musketeers. But with the Kings, at least you always know where you stand. They make everything look easy.

I got dreams. Two more years to college, and I already get letters in the mail from all the historically black colleges, not to mention the state schools and even an Ivy. I get straight A's, and my mom's had me taking the SAT since I was twelve, just for practice. She saves up for the fee every year, because the lady she cleans for said that's how her kid got into Harvard, high test scores. There's scholarships I can get, Mom says.

She's doing her best, but she doesn't really understand. She's lived on this block her whole life. She doesn't know being smart isn't enough. Working hard isn't enough. I gotta get real lucky, and before I even get a chance to be the right kind of lucky, I gotta get lucky enough to live.

I got dreams. I don't want to pack it up and settle into the streets.

But two whole years? That's a long damn time to go it alone.

MELODY

I kinda wanted to go to the funeral, but kinda not. So I came to visit Sheila instead. We watch the coverage on TV. Apparently, her brother didn't want her to attend the service, but there's a TV in her room and it's already on when I get there, which goes to show she does know what she's doing. She's not supposed to be watching, I bet.

She rocks toward the screen and away, staring quietly. People go in the church, come out. People make statements. Reporters. It's a bit of a snooze, actually, because the cameras don't go in the church.

When it's over, the steps flood with mourners leaving. The camera catches Brick, Noodle, and the 8-5 Kings exiting the church. Sammy's there. Sheila points at the screen and whimpers.

"What is it?" I ask.

Noodle gets up and starts speaking—there's a surprise. The other Kings cluster behind him in a bunched-up row of red.

Sheila points again, at the top left corner. All I see are Kings, but whatever she's spotted breaks the funereal mood, sure enough. She laughs and claps until the picture changes.

TINA

Ashes
Ashes
Dust
Dust
Some kind of funeral thing
Ashes
Ashes
Dust
Dust
Nana says the earth takes us back when we are finished
Ashes
Dust
Earth
None of those things is Tariq

REDEEMA

Tina screams and clings to the tall silver gates. Took one look at all the headstones, all the grass, and started bawling. Barely a word outta the preacher 'fore she bolted. Refuses now to step back inside the cemetery. Can't none of us get close enough to touch her.

Surely they've paused the service now, since we all went running after her.

"Tina, come on!" Vernie snaps. She tries again to pull Tina off the gate. Tina kicks her in the shins. Vernie smacks at the child's backside, like a reflex, but her hand just glances off.

Tina shrieks loud enough to curdle the blood of a ghost.

I pull my daughter back. "Don't make her."

My grandbaby's wailing, out of control. It'll be an hour before she has her head back. That tiny body is chock-full of stubborn. All of Vernie's and all of mine combined. Came by it honest.

"Them's hard gates to walk through," I remind Vernie. She just glares at me. But I know. I've had plenty of practice.

My job today is to hold Tina close, so Vernie can do what needs done. Not just today, come to think. This baby thrives on her Nana's magic touch. "You go on," I tell Vernie. "I'll stay with her. You go on and bury your boy."

We'll bury Tariq, and it'll be all right. I don't know how, Lord, but it'll be all right.

"Try to bring her up," Vernie says. "I want her to see. It's important." She kisses my cheek and follows the others.

Vernie and the rest of the family retreat across the grassy slope, toward the grave plot that was meant to be mine. We'll start saving for another one, soon as we can bear to. I got the feeling I'm gonna be around a while longer anyway. I'm needed here.

I watch till they disappear over the rise, then I heft my old bones down onto the sidewalk at the gates, close at hand but out of kicking range. Tina's screams die down to whimpers once there's no one left to impress. She's just like her brother—enjoys a good audience. *Ain't just a tantrum today, baby,* I want to say. *You got a right to scream like hell.* Tina looks to me, hands still sweatily gripping the bars. "We'll just wait right here," I promise. "Right here, baby."

Tina lets go of the bars and comes to me. She lies with her head on my thigh.

"You're saving me a long sad walk, baby girl," I tell her, smoothing back the hairs along the side of her face.

10. DUST TO DUST

REVEREND ALABASTER SLOAN

The soft knock at the door is something unholy. I know the rap of her knuckles—how do I know this? Because I am a low man. Low enough to have imagined this.

Emerging from prayer is like surfacing from underwater. It drips off me; it lingers.

Not long enough.

Not nearly.

I cross the carpet, gathering static, I suppose, with my sock feet. Move the chain, lever the handle, ring the DO NOT DISTURB tab with the crook of a finger.

The door opens. She stands there, all young and round, in that clingy gray dress. I lean forward, and she raises her face, but my gaze goes elsewhere for the moment. The hall is empty behind her. I have to take these things into account.

"Kimberly," I say.

"Reverend," she breathes, and it is a word like a firebrand stinging my skin.

"Call me Al," I answer. "We're friends now."

Friends.

She lowers her lashes and smiles. I step aside to allow her to pass, not so far aside, just enough that she can slip through the seam between my chest and the doorframe. She brushes me with her fullness, and I wonder what it means to be able to touch that kind of perfection. I hope I'm not about to spoil her with the wrongness that is smothering me. The promise of her company is the only thing keeping me standing.

"Of course. Al," Kimberly says. My name rolls off her tongue. She is killing me with her shy loveliness.

My room is a large bedroom suite, typical for me. When I have my staff in, we sit in the living area. They stay for hours; there is always work to be done. But I keep the bed closed off from them; some things are private. The bedroom door is open now, and I regret the oversight.

"Would you like a drink?" I offer, approaching the wet bar.

"Sure," she says. "Whatever you're having."

I mix up a pair of strong whiskey cocktails. She goes to the window, peeks out. She moves around the room freely this time, exploring the luxuries with the wonder of a child. But she moves like something else altogether. Stirring, I ask, "How old are you?"

"Nineteen," she says. Her fingers play along the gilded edge of the mirror above the bar. I swirl the whiskey, but I smell her perfume. "Almost twenty."

"Close enough." I smile, easing the drink toward her. She takes the glass with timid fingers. Sips.

"Hmm." She swallows half the liquid in a series of delicate gulps.

I drink in kind, surprised but willing.

KIMBERLY

"Let's talk about the next few days," Al says. I sit on the couch, and he pulls up a chair.

I take a small notebook out of my purse.

"In a couple of days, we're going to hold a demonstration calling for 'Justice for Tariq.'" He moves his hand through the air as if imagining a banner.

I take careful notes of the details he describes. Everyone will be asked to wear hooded sweatshirts. We will write press releases, organize speakers, post flyers, reach out on social media, and more.

He recites it all in a low, insistent voice. I'm on the couch, and he's in the chair alongside me. There is only one small light, over my shoulder.

I've been on dates, and this is how they go: drinks and a softly lit conversation.

It feels like any minute now, he's going to make a move. Instead, he walks me to the door.

TINA

Things I have found in Tariq's room:
>   Drawings I made for him
>   Homework, unfinished
>   A hundred and seventeen dollars

Wow. Plus:
>   Twelve dollars and ninety-four cents in coins
>   A postcard with Daddy's handwriting on it
>   A magazine with naked ladies—ha ha ha

Tariq has lots of secrets
>   Stinky dirty T-shirts—ick
>   Stinky dirty socks—double ick
>   Stinky dirty undies—triple ick

But there's no reason to wash them
>   A notebook with writing
>   My harmonica which he stole—I knew it
>   A knife as long as my elbow-to-wrist, with a red strap and a
>   smooth case of leather

Ouch
It is not a toy

REDEEMA

Tina comes crying. A gash in her hand and a palm full of blood.

"Child, what did you do?" I declare, scooping her against me. Can't get to the bathroom sink fast enough. It drips.

Water runs over the wound. Tina flinches. I steady her wrist under the flow.

"What happened, baby?"

"I cut myself," she says.

"On what?" It's a clean cut, swift and sure and deep enough that I start wondering how much them doctors charge you to sew up stitches.

Tina cries. Fat tears, the size of marbles.

The water washes away pink. I uncurl her hand, which opens the wound, but I got to see how deep. It's not so bad as it looked at first. I pour on peroxide till the whole line bubbles white. Tina whimpers and fidgets.

"It hurts."

"I know, sweet baby. I know."

In her palm, I stack up gauze drawn from the basket under the sink. Give her a round, thin perfume bottle to grip. "Squeeze tight, baby."

She fists up her hand. I fold my old fingers around hers. I got the arthritis these days. Can't put on that kind of pressure. But I gotta let her know I'm here. I'm always here.

TINA

"Mommy," I cry.

Uh-unh. Nana clucks at me. *Tell me what happened.*

"Mommy."

Hush. Your momma don't need to see more blood on her babies.

"Tariq," I cry.

Sweet baby, Nana says, *you know he ain't coming.*

"Tariq," I cry.

My hand feels bad.

My heart feels bad.

Tariq knows how to make things feel better.

JENNICA

The reporter and her cameraman come back into the diner. Her ponytail and her nosy smile haven't changed.

"I don't have anything else to say," I tell her. The camera rolls anyway. The black glassy eye seems to be looking right into me. Earlier, Noodle stood in front of a whole bank of cameras and told a story that I know he doesn't believe. He ranted over it all the way home, all lit up and energized. *Fucking Tariq. Who does he think he is? Dying and still coming back to be a pain in my ass.* Similar chorus to what I've been hearing all week, except his tone was less angry, now that he had a role to play in it. *Did you see me up there? You see what Brick's making me do?*

"You did good," I told him. He had a glow about him, almost like he was high. It was just the attention. All the lights and cameras. His ranting, just for show. He enjoyed himself up there. It makes me feel sick.

How can I talk to a reporter now? What if I say something that doesn't match what Noodle said?

"With all the new developments in the Tariq Johnson case, what are your thoughts about justice for Tariq?"

"I really don't have anything to say."

She pulls out her wallet, and I hold up my hands.

"I don't want to be on TV again," I insist. It calls too much attention. I just want to move on and forget the whole thing. If I work hard enough, maybe I can forget Tariq Johnson ever existed.

TYRELL

"Some reporter called today," Dad says over dinner. It's just the two of us tonight. Mom's working late.

"Yeah?"

He forks rice and beans into his mouth. "I don't want you talking to those people."

"I haven't."

"Well, don't."

"I said, I haven't."

"And I said, don't."

Dad used to smile at me. But it's been a long time.

We eat in silence for a while.

Dad says, "I don't want you getting tangled up in this Tariq mess."

"He was my best friend," I say. I'm as tangled as it gets.

11. WHAT'S NEXT?

BRIAN TRELLIS

I'm never going to get out from under this thing. I can say it a thousand times, and they just keep asking and asking again. I really thought he was armed.

"Thanks for coming in," Chip Castleman says. He flashes me his trademark high-wattage smile.

"I've never done anything like this. I'm not really sure what to say." The microphone clipped to my lapel is slipping. My fingers reach to straighten it, but Chip motions with a nod, and other hands take over for me, quick and efficient.

"Don't worry about it," he says. "It'll just be a few questions about the other day."

Additional lights snap on overhead and in front of me. All around, really. I blink into the brightness.

"This is your camera," a voice says in my ear. The chair beneath me swivels. "Look right there, okay?"

"Right where?"

From above: "We're live in five . . . four . . . three . . . two . . ."

"Good evening, ladies and gentlemen, I'm Chip Castleman. Thanks for joining us here on *Politics and Power*. Tonight we have the latest in the Tariq Johnson shooting investigation." He turns to me. "Thanks for joining us, Brian."

"Glad to be here, Chip." That sounded okay. But should I really be glad to be here? I'm not glad to be in this situation. *Glad* is the wrong word altogether.

Chip is still speaking.

"What was going through your mind when you intervened in a gang altercation?"

"Well, I don't know what it was, on that level," I say. "I heard Rocky—"

"The shopkeeper?"

"Right. I heard him shouting after Tariq, 'Stop, get back here.' So I tried to stop him from getting away."

"It seemed clear to you that he needed to be stopped?"

"Yeah. Well, I mean, Rocky was shouting. And it all happened so fast."

"Brian, it must have been terrifying to confront an armed gang member like that. What was going through your mind in those moments?"

"I—I didn't really have time to think, I guess."

"You just stepped up."

"I just stepped up."

"Words of a brave man, ladies and gentlemen. Thank you, Mr. Trellis. It's clear your actions might have prevented additional violence."

Is that clear? I wonder. *Gun,* someone shouted. But when I looked, I didn't see it. I'm sure it was there, but I can't remember actually seeing it.

The lights on me go dark. Chip continues on to some other guest. I've been waiting an hour. I may have to wait a while longer for the live recap. I'm never going to get out of here. Away from this.

TYRELL

Brick rolls down the block with his familiar swagger and a whole posse of 8-5s behind him. It's only ten blocks I have to walk, but right now it feels like a gauntlet. There's no realistic hope that they won't see me.

I keep my head down, but nothing doing.

"Oh, Ty-relllllllllll," Noodle calls in a singsong voice.

Tariq would have told me to just keep walking. He'd have had some words to toss at them. I only have numbers swirling in my head. Sixteen days left until summer. Third year in a row, I won a scholarship to science camp, way on the other side of the state. Six weeks out there, no 8-5s to worry about. Two years after that, before I go away to college. But by the fall, I'll get strong somehow. I'll find a way to resist like T did.

I just have to make it sixteen days.

"Yo, Tyrell," says Brick. "What's good?" He puts out his hand to slap skin with me. T woulda slapped. So I slap.

"Excuse me," I say. "I don't want to be late for school."

A few of the 8-5s snicker.

"Hey," Brick says, and they silence. "Our man Ty here's got a bright future. Someone's gotta take care of all the book learning."

"What's your GPA these days?" Noodle says.

I can't tell if they're making fun of me, or what. "Three point nine."

"Outta ten?" squeals Noodle. "Homes, I thought you's supposed to be a genius or some shit."

"Out of four." I try to skirt around them, but they're all over the sidewalk. I'd have to step into the street to get past, and then it'd be too obvious how bad I just want to get on my way.

"That's great, man," Brick says, in a voice that sounds almost serious. "Look, we don't want to mess anything up for you. We just want to let you know we're around."

As if I could forget.

"Why don't you come by my place tonight?" Brick says.

"No, thanks."

"You should come. It's a great party. Music. Refreshments. Plenty of honeys."

"You can get your little freak on," Noodle says, pumping his hips so the other guys laugh. At least now I know for sure they're teasing me.

"No," I say.

Brick slugs my arm. "Come on, man. I never seen you hanging with anyone but T. You even got other friends? What are you gonna do with yourself now?"

He coulda stabbed me; it wouldn't have hurt this bad. "I'm okay."

"You know we can hook you up with some easy coin too," says Noodle. "All them college applications."

"I'll get scholarships," I mumble. It burns, because I worry about it all the time.

"Homes, you know it costs money just to *apply* to them fancy schools."

"How would you know?" I blurt. I want to bite my tongue, but it's what T would have said. No holding back. For a second, I feel like he's with me. It doesn't make anything better. Because actually, he isn't.

Brick laughs, throws his arm around my shoulder. The other guys hoot, and start ragging on Noodle.

"Really, I don't—"

"It's just one party," Brick says. "Not a lifetime commitment."

I stay silent.

"You're coming," Brick insists. "Be out front of your building. We'll pick you up at nine."

They part and move on around me, down the block to the next stop on their harassment tour.

Sixteen days and counting.

TINA

Daddy's here.
Daddy's *never* here.
Count on the calendar:
Two years plus
Seven months plus
Nine days
Since he was here last.
One postcard to Tariq.
No postcards to me.
Mommy says, *Get the* BAD WORD *out!*
Daddy says, *Tina, sweetie, come to Daddy.*
Mommy says, *Get out right now.*
In a loud voice.
I cover my ears.
Daddy kneels down.
Don't you remember me?
Mommy says, *You leave her be.*
I don't forget.
I never forget.

REDEEMA

That fool thinks he can just waltz back in here, after all these years. He got another think coming.

Tina cries at the sight of him. That's right on, baby girl. The babies always know.

I know too. I know that man. I've seen. He walks in the door without knocking, like he owns the place. Like it's still home to him, when his hide ain't darkened our door for what? Two, three years? Didn't even bother to show his face at his own son's funeral.

Vernesha ain't having it. For a minute, she yells at him. But he wades right through. He's the calm *and* the storm, that one. When he folds her up in his arms, she sure enough lets him.

Lord, what are you doing to my babies? They's suffered enough.

VERNESHA

Mom reminds me that Terence has hurt me six ways to Sunday. As if I don't know. "Nothing but a shadow of a man," she says. "No substance."

I know his shadow well.

Terence never left this house; he was always in Tariq's face. In Tina's pencil drawings. I hate that I ever loved him, hate even more that I can't be rid of him because of how they carry him, and they are everything to me. He has their love but never has to do the hard things. In his shadow state, he hovers over us, a thousand times removed. Every meal I served. Every cut I ever kissed. Every time I had to answer "Why doesn't Daddy love us?"

I know he can't feel what I feel. Like a piece of my heart has been carved out and set on fire. But he has to feel something. That's his son, too.

My father died young. Mom raised us without him; she's a force of nature. I'm not like that, although I've had to be. She just doesn't get it—a man is good for some things.

The kitchen faucet has dripped for two years. "Fix it," I tell Terence. He does.

A guilty man is good for even more things. "Go get us some coffee," I tell him. He goes.

Door closes behind him, and Mom starts in. "That man," she wails. "That man! Who does he think he is?"

She doesn't need to worry about me kicking him out. I've

learned the lesson enough times. Hard. He never sticks around. It's only for a little while.

"That bastard," Mom thunders. "He just wants a piece of the limelight. He too twisted to see that kind of attention ain't worth the air it traveled through."

"I know, Mom." But I want fresh coffee, and I don't want to leave the house. He wants the cameras, he can have them. They're waiting out there, like rats.

We had rats in the building last summer. Where was he?

We drove three hours to meet a new doctor for Tina the winter before that. Where was he?

Well, he's here now, and damned if I'm not going to use him.

"You gotta fight this, Vernie," Mom says. "You can't let him in like this."

The pain constricts my chest. Out of nowhere, like it happens.

"My baby is dead!" I scream at her. My fingers claw the back of the couch. For a while, I can't breathe. For a while, I don't know. I don't know. I can't. I'm not going to make it.

When I come up, Mom is holding me. We are heaped on the floor. My face is wet, my skin and bones are shaking. There is no way forward. There is only this.

"Okay, Vernie," Mom says. "Let it out, baby."

"All the fight I got in me," I tell her, "is just to get through this."

REVEREND ALABASTER SLOAN

This Terence Johnson character embodies everything that's wrong with our communities. In and out of his children's lives, even though he has a job and a place and, by all accounts, some sense of right and wrong. He scurries from the building as I'm getting out of my cab. I jump back in, tell the cabbie to keep rolling until he's down the block a ways. Let's skip the press on this occasion.

Johnson holds his head down, tucks his jacket collar in like it isn't summer. He recognizes me when I get out of the cab and walk toward him, but he tries to duck away.

"Let's take a walk," I say to Tariq's father.

"I'm headed to pick up some coffee for Vernesha," he says, still trying to dodge me.

"Well, I can come along for that."

"I'm not asking for company."

We walk farther than I expect. Past at least a dozen places likely to sell coffee. Maybe he's trying to outwalk me. I keep pace and get him chatting about small topics. Not the main concern on both our minds. He leads me into a small diner.

"Vernesha likes the coffee at this place," he says. "It's worth the walk."

I'm surprised at that layer of consideration. By all accounts, he could be better. A better man, a better father. Instead of looking out for his own needs all the while. Does it make all his absences worse, maybe, knowing he's capable of thinking beyond himself, even in the smallest of ways?

I try not to judge people; there's a plank in my own eye sure enough. But these children deserved better.

KIMBERLY

I'm not familiar with the diner where Al asks me to meet. I've passed by it a hundred times, I'm sure, but I've never been inside.

Tucked under my arm is the paperwork for him. He's sitting alone in a window booth, making his way through a plate of meat loaf and mashed potatoes. It's a time for comfort food, sure enough.

"You want something to eat?" Al says.

"All right."

The waitress comes over with water and a menu. I glance up, just with a smile and thanks. It's Jennica. I did her hair the other day.

"Hi, Jennica."

"Hi, Kimberly. I came to your job—now you're at mine." She smiles, and I feel like she means it, but the expression is not convincing.

"How are you doing?" I ask.

She shrugs, her eyes distant and haunted. She stands too long beside our table.

"It'll get better," I tell her, pressing her hand.

"I don't know," she says. "Isn't there always something?"

JENNICA

When it gets hard to handle what has happened, I remind myself I didn't really know Tariq. I just knew him to say hi to. We went to the same school, though he's two years behind me. Was.

I don't have stories about him. He doesn't fit anywhere in the photo album of my life up until now, barely even a blur in the background or on the fringe of some forgotten frame. There's just this one thing that binds us.

I was leaning over him when he died. My hands on his chest. My palms felt his last breath move inside him. His chest rose and fell and then kept falling, like it could carry us both straight down through the earth.

I didn't stop pushing, but I knew. Right then. I was breathing hard myself. My lungs probably took in the last air Tariq ever exhaled. It can't possibly be in me anymore, but it feels like it is. Like it's weighing heavy on my chest with every breath I take, even now.

That's it. That's all we have. No other memories. No previous touch to cover up the feel of his hand against my arm, lightly clutching. No long-ago look to take the place of the desperate glance we shared, or the hollow stare from his dark, empty eyes an instant later.

My lips never so much as brushed his cheek before. Nothing to eclipse the kiss I refused to give him that would have been his last . . . or could have saved him. His breath is in my chest, still now, and I never even tried to give it back to him.

12. SHARP THINGS

TYRELL

It turns out I don't remember everything. That's just how memories are, I guess, and it never bothered me before, but it does now. Because usually, when you forget how something went, you turn to someone and go, *Remember that time we . . .* And they remember it, and they help you fill in the blanks.

With T there was this one time—we were maybe thirteen or fourteen, so it wasn't even all that long ago—when we scored a bag of small orange balloons from somewhere. I can't remember how we got them, but that's not a big deal, that kind of detail. Anyway, we took them up to the roof of my building. We filled them with water first, and we had plastic grocery bags full of them. Lugging them up there was no picnic, but we got a whole arsenal of them and started throwing them down at other kids.

We did a few grown-ups, too, although we avoided throwing them at the Kings.

We must have been up there for a couple of hours, because we were being real choice about who we went after and how we aimed, and we had to duck and cover after each shot to be sure no one could figure out where exactly it came from.

I remember all of this like yesterday. If I close my eyes I can feel the warm hand of the sun on my back, the whisper of wind through my neck hairs, which stood on end at every shot. I remember the glow of T's wide smile and how, deep in my stomach, I was afraid we were going to get caught and hauled off the roof by my dad or someone even worse. In the middle of it, though, that underbelly feeling didn't really matter, because of how good it all felt. The weight of each balloon, perfect in my palm, full but soft enough to squeeze and mold and play with.

T did most of the throwing. That's just who he was, always in charge. Mostly I held the balloons and handed them to him and helped him pick out targets. I was fine with that—it was part of what made us work as friends. And anyway, I liked holding the balloons. I'd never felt a girl's breast before, but I figured it might be kinda like that, based on the shape and the bounce and whatnot. Neither of us had much experience in that area, actually. So I made a joke about how, with T's track record with girls, he maybe should think twice about throwing all these boobs away, and T laughed. I wasn't usually the funny one or the one who brought up anything to do with girls, and the look on T's face gave me props for going there.

But of course, being the funny one, he one-upped me right away. He said something back, something that was so funny we stopped with the balloons for like ten minutes and just lay on the gravel rooftop laughing our asses off. The kind of laugh that makes you think you're gonna die because you can't get a breath in. The kind of laugh that clenches your gut and works off calories like it's exercise. The kind of joke that makes you laugh the same way two years later, just thinking of it.

Except, I can't remember what it was that he said. For the life of me, I can't.

JENNICA

"You look thin," my auntie Anjelica says. I'm just passing through the kitchen on my way back to work. She's bent over the potted plants in the kitchen windowsill, watering them and putting her face so close it's like she's thinking of licking their leaves or something.

She's right. My uniform doesn't feel as tight as usual. I haven't really been eating these past few days.

"What are you doing?" I ask.

"The begonia is not well," she answers, stroking one plump bud near its stem. "Eat some chicken before you go. And some rice and beans. I'll make you a tamale. What do you want?"

"I have to go. I don't have time."

"Always time to eat!" she declares. She whisks chicken and rice out of the fridge. By the time I'm at the door, she's standing in front of me with a cold plate under my nose. They should hire her at the diner.

"It's no good cold," she says. "You wait. I heat."

"That's okay," I tell her. "You know I work at a restaurant, right?"

Anjelica clucks as she pops the plate in the microwave. "You don't need to buy any food. We have food right here." She punches the buttons, and the whirring sound begins.

"I have to go."

"What would your mother say?"

"My mother knew food doesn't fix everything." Immediately I feel bad for snapping at her. But I can't help myself. "It's not magic."

Anjelica eyes me in that furious way, looking just like my mother did when she was mad. But instead of flinging angry words, she takes my face in her hands. "Then you are not eating the right food," she says. The microwave hums.

"I'm not hungry," I tell her as I slip out the door.

KIMBERLY

It's harder than it should be to knock on that door. And strange having to wade through the gaggle of press still camped out in front of the Johnsons' building. They're not interested in me, though; I slip inside without even causing a blip on their radar. The inner door is propped, so I just head for the stairs and start climbing.

Tariq's greatma answers the door. In the kitchen behind her, something's simmering on the stove, and she just looks at me for a while like she's trying to place me. Suddenly it all feels like the worst kind of intrusion.

"I'm sorry," I stammer. "I just came to pay my respects."

"That's all right, child," Redeema says. "Thank you."

Tina scampers in. Maybe she recognized the sound of my voice, but anyway, before I can excuse myself and slink away, the little girl throws her arms around me and buries her face in my middle.

"I guess you'd better come in," Redeema says. Not unwelcoming, just matter-of-fact.

"Yes, come in." Tina spins away and rushes into the living room. "Kimberly's here!" she announces. "You can all go away now."

I hear laughter from the next room, male and female. Leave it to a child to bring humor even in tragedy. I can't help but smile myself. The expression freezes on my face, though, as I cross through the doorway and, sitting in the living room alongside Vernesha, is Al.

"Uh, hello, Reverend Sloan."

"Hi, Kimberly," he says. A hint of surprise flashes across his face. Maybe I should have told him I was thinking of stopping by.

I drag my eyes away and look at Vernesha. "I'm sorry, I didn't mean to intrude."

"No intrusion," she says. "You've met the Reverend Sloan?"

"Kimberly has been kind enough to help me with a bit of makeup for my television appearances. And she's been assisting with some administrative duties while I'm in town." He turns to me. "Vernesha and I were just discussing the upcoming demonstration."

"Do you think people will come?" Vernesha says, looking at me. I can't imagine her heartache, amid the craziness going on outside—in the press and in the neighborhood.

"Yes," I say honestly. "Everyone is very upset about what happened. Especially how it happened." I cringe inside, wondering if it sounded like I meant the circumstances were more upsetting to people than Tariq's actual death. Maybe it is that way, but I wouldn't have meant to say it to his mother.

Tina's small hand slips into mine, begins tugging. I'm already off balance, so she gets me moving easy.

"Nice to see you, Reverend."

He smiles warmly. "Likewise."

"Tina, the adults are talking," Vernesha says. "Wait just a minute." The girl's trying to pull me toward her bedroom. Which makes sense, I guess, because we used to play in there a lot.

"It's okay," I say. "I came to see how she's doing. Anyway, you already have company."

"Thank you, Kimberly."

"Come on," Tina commands. She stomps to the other side of me and starts leaning with her whole weight against me.

"Okay, sweetie. I'm coming."

Al and Vernesha watch us go, and I wonder what he thinks of me, going off to play. Will he see me as a child now? Did he already?

I sit on the edge of Tina's neatly made bed. She's always been such a good cleaner. I never had to cajole her to get her to put her toys away. Now she goes to the closet shelves and pulls out a well-worn box of Chutes and Ladders. We set it up on the rug.

One of her hands is not as useful as usual. It's all bandaged up across the palm.

"What happened to your hand?"

"I cut myself," she tells me, holding it up. "It was gross."

"Ouch."

"Yes."

"I'm sorry about Tariq."

"People say sorry all day."

"I bet they do."

"They didn't all hurt Tariq, did they?" she says.

I half smile. I've always thought there should be a different word for it too. "It's not always an apology. Sometimes it's sympathy."

She nods.

"When they say 'I'm sorry,' they really mean 'I feel sad just like you do.' "

"There was only one man who hurt Tariq," she says.

"That's right."

"He didn't say sorry."

"No," I agree. "He certainly didn't."

TINA

Kimberly does not ask what I cut my hand on;
I don't have to tell a lie.
I lied to Nana, like a bad girl:
"I tried to use the grown-up scissors."
Let's go clean them and put them away.
"I was putting them away when I cut myself."
Nana pulled the scissors out of the drawer and rinsed them.
They were already clean but
She believed me anyway.
Hee hee.
I am in trouble for touching sharp things now,
but I feel proud for coming up with such a good lie.
Tariq always said lies were bad,
but it turns out he was good at them, too.

13. RIDE-ALONG

TYRELL

All of a sudden, it seems like everyone's an 8-5 King. I sit on the steps out in front of my building, and I'm trying to think about who I can go to and ask them, *How'd you stay out? You know, what did you say when the 8-5s rolled around?* But there's no one I can think of that I know well enough to lay it out for them and try to figure a way through this.

It's just one party. Not a lifetime commitment. But every notch is a step closer to the whole ball of wax, and what if someday I wake up all dressed in red with a knife under my pillow and I look back and go, *If only I'd blown off Brick that night . . .*

Crap.

It's the beginning of the end already, isn't it? But to blow off

Brick means bringing down a rain of trouble. He'll be on me every day. I know it.

T went to some of Brick's parties. He'd get invited, kinda the same way it happened to me. He told me what it's like. Dancing. Drinking. Girls. I think he started to enjoy it, after a while. I can't pretend I'm not curious, too.

One time, when we were kids, before he ever went to a Kings party, T came over to my house. He had this look on his face. Sneaky, like he was up to no good. Which usually meant something fun was about to happen.

"Check it." Tariq pulled a six-pack of cans from behind his back. It was a four-pack, actually—he had it dangling by two empty rings. Miller Genuine Draft.

"Whoa," I said. "Where'd you get that?"

Neither of us had ever tried beer before. Probably none of our friends had yet, either. Junior claimed his dad let him drink it at home, but not while anyone else was around, so we had no evidence to back this up. I didn't know about Sammy, but likely not. His mom had him up in the Baptist church on Sundays and Wednesdays, just like mine. I'd never seen a drop of alcohol in our apartment.

"I found it," Tariq said. He pulled one ring free and tossed the can to me.

"You found it?" The beer in my hand felt suddenly suspect. I wasn't about to drink some mysterious street brew.

"My dad had buddies over last night," he said. "These four

cans just kinda walked away." He made little walking motions with his fingers.

"You're such a punk," I told him.

"Come on." Tariq grinned. "We gotta break your geek cherry sometime."

"Cheers." We clinked the cans. It didn't make much of a sound, but I wanted to look over my shoulder anyway.

The beer was warm and foamy in my mouth. Pretty gross. It took an effort to swallow. We sat quiet for a while, sort of chewing it. We each took down a couple of sips.

"Are you drunk?" Tariq said.

"I think so," I answered. So we put the rest of the cans under my bed and hid them behind a pile of books.

We were such huge idiots back then. It's funny. If Tariq was here, and I reminded him about that time, we would laugh for an hour. It's hard to laugh over anything without him.

We were the holdouts. For the longest time, it kept us together. We were a gang of two. And that was always enough.

SAMMY

Riding low in the back of Noodle's Chevy is such a freaking rush. I'm running with the big dogs now. It's headier than the sweet MJ that clogs my throat.

They come by my place, and Brick goes, "Come along with us." Of course I go. No question.

I'm alone in the back seat. They're piled in the front: Noodle, Jennica, and Brick. We drive awhile, then the car slows. Brick lays his arm across the seat. His fingers pass through the curtain of Jennica's hair as he turns toward me.

"You know him, right?" Brick says. "Help him come around."

Out the window I see where we are. The last person I'd expect to see comes walking toward the car. Slow, like a convict on the way to the electric chair. He slides in next to me, stiff as a wall, with eyes round and shadowed as the moon.

My chest pulses with some deep energy. *No, no.* My heart beats. *No, no.*

"Hey, Ty," we all say.

"Hey," he says. His eyes meet mine, and for one dragging moment, it's just the two of us. I've looked into his eyes so many times over the years that I can read him. He's beyond his depth and scared. But he'll come around. Like we all do.

Help him come around, Brick said.

Is this all Brick wants me for? To somehow get to Ty? I don't know the first thing to say to him. I can't even remember the last time we talked. Wait, I do remember. It was like a year ago. He was with Tariq, of course. It was outside Junior's trial, and me and T was kinda sparring over T being pretty sure Junior didn't do the murder he went down for. At least not by himself. I told T, *Shut up—Junior did it*, because it's the last thing I wanted to think about, then or now: how people don't usually get what they deserve.

Ty's hand flips over, palm up, on the center seat between us. I think maybe he wants me to take hold of it. Like we used to when we were little.

But I don't.

Nothing's like it was. T gone and Junior locked up, and Ty and me just picking up the pieces. Our pact from the old days has been pounded into sand.

That's the other thing I see when Ty looks at me. The sharp sting of blame. Isn't that the pot now, calling the kettle black? We're both in this car. Both rolling down the same dark road.

It was always going to be like this, wasn't it?

No one ever keeps that kind of promise. I don't know why I'm surprised.

JENNICA

It's the same exact ride as every other time we've done this. Cruising the edge of King territory, pumping the volume with the bass on full, looking for Stingers who might be stepping out of line.

You have to drink or smoke a lot before it gets fun, and I'm sober after a long afternoon at the diner. I haven't been eating much, and I've learned my lesson about drinking on an empty stomach. I almost still feel sick from the last time. But I can't make myself get hungry, so I'm going to be good, even though it *is* kind of nice to just check out and get wasted.

The guys smoke joints with the windows cracked and the fan on high to diffuse the smell in case we get pulled over. Except we never get pulled over, because no one, including the cops themselves, would put it past Brick to ice a cop to get himself out of a ticket.

Noodle brakes the car at a red light. Corner of Pear and Roosevelt.

"Whoa, what the hell, what the hell?" Brick says. Sammy leans forward to see, and I feel his breath on the back of my neck. The hairs stand up there. Not because of him.

A block ahead, on Onerfin Avenue, a big group of Stingers is gathering across the street. Noodle slows the car.

"They're about to step on our turf," Sammy cries. "What the fuck is that?"

"If they cross the street, they're asking for it," Noodle says.

My heartbeat picks up, and I'm more freaked out than I ought to be. I've seen them throw down with the Stingers dozens of times. Usually it's words. Sometimes they show their knives. No one actually crosses the line, unless it's to start trouble.

We haven't had an all-out war in a year. Now isn't the time to start one, either. Not with me and Ty in the car. And not with all the press heat on us. On the Kings, I mean. But it might be a good time from the Stingers' perspective. I swallow hard.

The light turns green. "Are we getting into it?" Noodle asks.

"They're on the borderline," Brick says. "Gotta let 'em know we know." He cranks the window handle. Noodle's car is so old, it doesn't have power windows. I don't know why that bothers me—except, I guess, this whole cruising thing is so damn old.

"Yo, roll down my window," Sammy says.

"Roll it yo damn self," Noodle mutters.

Sammy laughs. "I forgot." Then he and Brick both hang their arms out the windows, knives flipped open and showing.

"One more step, and we slice you," Brick shouts. The Stingers rush to the edge of the sidewalk. They lift up their yellow jerseys and hoodies and show that they've all got holstered daggers tied at their waists. The infamous "Stingers."

"Slice you up real nice," Sammy calls. "Like bacon."

Brick, Noodle, and Sammy howl with laughter. Noodle slams the gas, jerking my head back, flaring up the sore spot in my neck that I thought was healing.

"That shit was close," Sammy hoots.

"Oh, God," Tyrell whispers. In the rearview, I see him gripping the door handle with one fist, clutching his own thigh with the other.

"They've got a mess coming to them now," Noodle answers. "What we gonna do?"

"Circle around," Brick says. "And get ready to jump."

My own voice screams in my head. *I don't want to be here.*

TYRELL

I'm gonna die tonight. I don't know why I didn't realize it before. One party? No commitment? My ass. My stupid, about-to-die ass.

At least it'll all be over, and I won't have to struggle anymore. I close my eyes, lean my head back against the car seat, and wait for the bullets to get me.

But the next thing I hear is Brick and them laughing. "Punk-ass Stingers. Yellow to the core."

I open my eyes. We've come around the corner again, and the cluster of Stingers is gone. Back around the buildings, safe on their own hallowed ground.

My fists are squeezed so tight it's painful. I dry my palms on my thighs.

I guess I got lucky.

JUNIOR

I was proud the day I joined the Kings. Wore my colors. Got my knife. I feel a bit naked now without those things. After a year in the life, it's hard to get comfortable in my bland gray prison clothes.

Most guys around here find ways of showing colors. King for life. No shaking it. Maybe I'll start wearing colors again someday, if I feel like it.

There's a lot of *ifs* in life, Mom used to say. She always had her head in the clouds. Saved a dollar every week for a lotto ticket, but we never won more than twenty. That was a banner week around the Collins household. We had Chips Ahoy for dessert every night and Pop-Tarts after school. That's what I remember.

That, and Mom always saying what else was going to happen, *if we win big this week.*

Mom's *ifs* were always about the future. Mine are all about the past.

If I hadn't joined the Kings.

If I hadn't trusted Sciss and taken the rap. I believed him when he said, *You'll only do a few years. You're a juvie. Easiest way to get made.*

If the guy hadn't died. He wasn't supposed to. Sciss beat him too hard after I cut him. It was only supposed to be a warning. The beating's what killed him. And when he died, Sciss disappeared.

If my court-appointed lawyer had really listened. They showed pictures in court of my online profile—me with my knife. *Where's the knife now?* they kept asking. *You disposed of it after the fact,* they insisted. I didn't, but what was I supposed to do, put it forward as evidence against myself?

That's why I gave my knife to T to keep. It's ironic now, how everyone's talking about him the exact same way: *Were you armed, Tariq Johnson? Where's the gun, Tariq Johnson?* Even without it, they still find a way to convict.

TYRELL

After a near-death experience, it feels like anything's possible. It feels like what happens next doesn't matter because it was supposed to be over right then. The Stingers were supposed to rush the car and shoot us, and I was supposed to follow Tariq into the easy quiet spaces of death. But I'm still here.

I breathe hard for a while, and Sammy finally goes, "It's okay, man. Calm down."

"I can't," I whisper, because I've been scared down to my bones and it doesn't wash off that fast.

Sammy hands me his joint, and I take it between my fingers. I could have died.

I don't know what to do with it.

"Just sip it in," Sammy says. "Hold it in your lungs. You're gonna feel better."

I do it like he says, and I come up coughing.

"Again."

I do.

We pile out of Noodle's car in front of Brick's place, and everyone is floating high. Except me, of course, although I breathed on Sammy's joint a couple of times. A bunch of times, maybe. I don't know anymore.

Two puffs, or three, or . . . I cover my mouth and laugh behind my hand.

Was it only a minute ago, or a while? It didn't taste like it smells, and it needled my throat. *Needles in my throat? What does that mean?* I didn't like it at first. But now I don't care. Because I could have died, so it doesn't matter. Nothing matters.

I laugh again. Brick puts his arm around me. "There you go," he says. "You feel better, don't you?"

"Yeah, kinda," I admit. "It's not so bad."

"I knew you'd come around," he says. "Next thing is, we gotta find you a girl."

"Naw." Girls never want anything to do with a nutball little numbers freak like me. They let me help them with their homework, and that's about all. I don't mind, though. I get to smell them and sit real close to them, and sometimes while they lean in and concentrate, I can see right down their shirts. They smile at me a lot. It's not nothing.

"It's no problem. Yo, Aimee," Brick calls, and this beautiful girl spins out of the mosh pit and glides toward us. "This is Tyrell."

"Hey, Tyrell," she purrs. She grabs my hand and presses herself against my side, liquid and warm and sweet. "You gonna dance with me?" She draws me forward, toward the crush and the noise.

I look back at Brick.

"You can have it like this," he says. "Every night."

It wouldn't be so bad.

14. DARK

KIMBERLY

Al says he's working, but he's not. The file folders are open on his lap, but he isn't reading them. He's staring at his own sock feet propped up on the coffee table. And stroking his bottom lip with a thumb.

My fingers click over the keys of his laptop. He's given me a list of media outlets to email with his latest press release. One by one, he says, with their name at the top. Gets better results when they think it's personal. I'm emailing folks at CNN, MSNBC, the networks, local and regional affiliates. Big-league stuff.

My attention is divided. He hasn't moved in about half an hour. "Are you all right?" I ask.

He stirs. "It was sweet of you to come and play with the little girl."

"Tina? I just thought probably no one makes a point of visiting her. So I did."

"You're very thoughtful." His smile reaches across the short space between us.

"She has no one to play with now. She looked up to him so much. She was always going, 'Tariq does this,' and 'Tariq says' whatever it might be."

"It caught me by surprise, seeing you."

"I didn't know you'd be there. I could have come another time."

He frowns. "I didn't mean that it bothered me."

"Okay."

He settles into silence. I stretch my arms and stand. Carry the laptop to the armchair nearer him. After two hours sitting at that desk, working, I don't think it's obvious I just want to get closer to him.

"You seem distracted," I say.

"Uh . . . I was thinking about my son, I guess."

"I've seen him on TV." He's my same age, I know that much, but it doesn't seem like a good thing to mention.

"We have now . . . ," he starts. "We don't really . . . He keeps his distance from me."

"Sorry," I say, which makes me think of Tina. Why isn't there a better word? Sympathy is its own thing.

"He was always a really good kid. Like Tariq."

I tip my head away. It wouldn't be right to say anything.

Al looks at me. "You don't think so?"

I shrug. "It's not my place."

"Tell me."

I pick at the chair arm. "He wasn't so nice. Everyone's making him out to be some kind of angel."

"That always happens when someone dies. People put on rose-colored glasses and talk about the good times."

"I guess."

"Maybe he was an asshole. It doesn't change what I'm doing here. He still didn't deserve to die that way."

"No, of course not. But he was kind of . . . I feel bad for saying it."

Al smiles. "Don't be afraid to speak the truth. It matters," he says, almost wistful.

"Isn't that what you're doing, when you go out there?"

"Not necessarily," he says. "It's bigger than me. Bigger than you, or Tariq, too."

He reaches for the remote control and changes the channel. He watches the news like it's part of his religion. It's still muted, but probably not for much longer.

I wonder what he would do if I went and sat beside him. If I were to curl against his side or lay my head on his thigh. Would he let me slide my fingers between his shirt buttons? Would he bring his hand down to touch me, or would he just push me away?

REVEREND ALABASTER SLOAN

It's late at night. Much too late to be alone in my hotel room with a girl who amounts to little more than an intern. Especially one who looks at me with those youthful, longing eyes and tugs me to talk about my feelings.

"Would you like another drink?" I offer, which only serves to dig me in deeper. There's too much to be done in advance of the march we're organizing. No time for a detour.

"Sure," she says.

I pour. Kimberly's eyes shine in the reflection of the flashing TV screen. It makes her look like she's on fire. I try to forget she kissed me once, entirely unprovoked. Or maybe she simply picked up on the truth: that I wanted it. I'm not so blameless.

I could reach for her here and now, and she'd come willingly. But she's too young. Too innocent. And already too attached.

She smiles up at me, and I dare to brush a stray wisp of hair from her cheek as I hand her a cocktail.

"You're lovely," I say. It just slips out. "How are the emails coming?" I down my drink too fast. Pour another while she gives me her status report.

JENNICA

It's no different than usual, being at Brick's place, smoking and drinking. It's pretty much all Noodle ever wants to do. Except sometimes we drive around again after, riding in Brick's car, usually, and cranking the music so loud the *thumpa thumpa* sets the car lurching on its tires.

It didn't bother me before. It's just that now, since Tariq, everything feels like it's moving in a big circle. Like the same things are happening over and over.

Get up, go to school, go to work, let Noodle pick me up, go to Brick's place, hope tonight's not the night they decide to get into it with the Stingers. Get up, go to school, go to work . . .

At Brick's, I stare out the window at the mural painted on the metal security door of a shop, the kind that opens like a garage door, one panel at a time, and disappears into the ceiling when the place is open. I look down at this piece a lot. It's one of those art pieces that disappears with the daylight and comes back each night, a memorial for some King who got knifed and killed by a Stinger some months back. His name was Scoot. So says the paint across the metal. I didn't know him. Maybe that doesn't matter, except it feels significant. Because for all the times I stand here with these guys, I don't really know them. Except Noodle and Brick. And the closer I get, the less I like what I see.

So I look at the mural, to remember how there's always more

than what I'm looking at. Some of it's good—maybe we woulda been friends, Scoot and me. No way to know.

Some of it's bad. Knives, death, always living on edge. First Scoot. Now Tariq. There's going to be another, and another. A great big terrible circle.

Some of it's inevitable, maybe. The rest just happens.

WILL (AKA eMZee)

It's been almost a week, and no one's done it. I guess that means they're all waiting on me. I woulda let it go this time, if someone else had taken the initiative, but it stands to reason. This is the kinda respect I guess I've earned.

Standing up top comes with a price, though. It means I got to be the one to decide how these walls remember Tariq Johnson. I got to be the one to speak his legacy on the face of the 'hood.

I woulda done it on day one, but it wasn't my place to step into it. I don't tag for the Kings, or the Stingers either. I'm my own man out here. I paint in gray, black, and white for a reason.

Every night, I've been looking for a piece done up by Spittz or JDog, the top guys who tag for the Kings. Thought they'd be tripping over themselves to memorialize one of their own. For once, the place to put it is obvious. Nice of Tariq to get mowed down just about smack in front of a big blank wall.

When I mural, I do landscapes or portraits, not much else. I don't do words. I don't get sappy, I don't get political. It's my art, just a way to put myself out there.

A portrait of Tariq might end up seeming political, but I just gotta do what I do, and try to get it right. I take the gray can in my left hand, the white in my right. At my feet are mounds of burned-out candle wax, fistfuls of dying flowers blown by the wind and roughed by the ravages of the street. Handwritten messages: *Love you, Tariq. Our hearts follow you always. We miss you already. Crying 4 U.*

What has happened here surrounds me, starts to fill me. I let it in, so it can find its way out onto the wall. Breathe into it. Breathe. Tagging is light work. But this is heavy.

Who were you, Tariq Johnson?

The question makes me smile. I tip my wrists. Ball bearings knock against the insides of the cans. My wrists move faster. Tariq Johnson can be whoever I want him to be. Here and now. Memorialized.

My arms arc over my head. The vision bursts in front of me; I never know what I'm painting till I start. My feet nudge aside the vigil remnants, giving me more room to work.

The rattle of the cans. The hiss of the spray. That tangy liquid scent that just about gets me high. A meditation.

REVEREND ALABASTER SLOAN

I'm letting Tariq's death get to me in a way it shouldn't. Drinking, barely working, letting Kimberly stay.

I pour another drink. It's all right. Away from the cameras, the work doesn't require me to be at peak form. I've planned several dozen memorial marches; I can do it in my sleep. That isn't the point.

Why, this time, is it burrowing inside me? I wake up each morning to find my polling numbers up. I should be happy. I stopped, some time ago, *feeling* for each lost child. It's just not possible. Grieving would become the majority of my job, in that case. You can't sustain that kind of sorrow. Tariq Johnson's death, while tragic, is no more tragic than any of the others I've confronted. Why do I feel this pain?

Kimberly sighs lightly. From time to time, she rubs herself, unconsciously, beneath her breast. It has become my favorite mannerism. Watching her helps me fight the desire to call my son just to listen to him breathing. Kimberly bends over the keyboard intently. Her shoes are off now, stockinged toes hooked over the lip of the coffee table. Every inch of her is sexy beyond belief. Time to send her on her way, before the night gets any longer.

Except I can't stop looking.

"What is your dream?" I ask Kimberly, which is more or less the opposite of asking her to leave. "What is it that you want?"

"I don't know," she says, striking the keyboard as if finishing a thought. She stretches her arms and looks at me. I must appear as a heap of a man to her, unpleasantly lumped on the sofa.

"I mean, if you could have anything," I clarify. It's so easy to trip toward the fantastic. What I could be, what I could have, what I'd do with all the money and power in the world if it was handed to me. How good I could be. How happy.

"I'd like to be able to set my own hours at the salon."

I laugh. "No, come on. I mean, if money's no object. You ask for it, it's yours."

She gazes at me quietly, with nothing to add. I see something powerful in her eyes, powerful, but contained. Even her wildest dreams are limited.

"Anything in the world," I urge her. "No boundaries." I'm expecting her to say be president, or an astronaut, or a film star, or a billionaire CEO, or the queen of a tropical isle.

"Maybe to have my own salon one day," she says.

I close my eyes. "Yes. You could have that. Absolutely."

"I doubt it."

My chest crushes in on itself. Yet again, I am reminded of how my generation has failed to instill in our children what is truly possible.

"Kimberly," I whisper, "hasn't anyone ever told you how amazing you are? You can be anything you want to be. In the real world."

She ducks her head. "I don't come from that world," she says.

Maybe not. Compared to the world I'm used to, she seems so pure and innocent. So clean.

I push myself to my feet, headed back to the bar, but I stumble. My fingers graze the arm of the couch, and like a shot, she sets the laptop aside and is there with me.

"You okay?" she whispers, stepping into the circle of my arms.

"I guess I've had enough."

"It's a hard week." She makes an allowance for me, though there's really no excuse. I don't deserve this comfort, but hell itself could not drag me from it.

Kimberly snuggles closer, and I hold her against me, surer than ever that it was a bad mistake to draw her in like this. Just because I like the smell and the feel and the spirit of her doesn't mean I have the right to hold her like this.

KIMBERLY

It's not going to last forever, I remind myself.

The hotel mirror is perfectly clean, but for the echo of a few rag swipes in the top left corner. I lean on the speckled counter, put my face close to the reflection.

He lives in Washington. You live here.

He's famous. You're a nobody.

I'm not an idiot. I know how the world works. I watch TV. Guys like Al fly in and tease your dreams, then leave. I do know that.

But he's been so incredibly sweet to me. We drink the finest liquor; room service is like a five-star buffet. Even if you order a burger and fries, it comes with the most adorable little ketchup bottles, three inches tall. Al noticed that I like them, so he started ordering extra so I can put them in my purse. I have a lot of them at home now, lined up like soldiers across the front of my dresser. That's the kind of person he is. So, so sweet.

"Kim?" he says, from the other room. "You all right?" I only walked in here to get us each a glass of water. We used the kitchenette cups for the other drinks.

"Coming," I call. I run the water, finally.

It's not going to last forever.

But when I look in the mirror, I can't help seeing it. The two of us walking on a road that doesn't end. I imagine looking over my shoulder one morning to find Al gazing at me in that sweet way. "Come with me back to Washington," he'll say. I'll pretend I have to think about it. Keep him in suspense. But the answer would already be in my heartbeat. *Of course. Of course.*

People need their hair cut everywhere, right? Maybe he would put me on his staff, as his makeup artist. I would go everywhere he goes. And sometimes, after a long day's work, he would come to my small, well-decorated apartment instead of going home. I know how the place would look, even. What I would put on the walls and the sort of furniture I would buy. I have some savings already. I could do that, and he would be impressed by how fast I made an empty place look like home. He would want to come by more and more often, just to be there. With me.

I shut off the water, and in the sudden quiet it all seems so stupid. I'm smarter than that. I know what happens to politicians' girlfriends in Washington. I watch TV.

Girlfriend, ha. Get your head out of the clouds, girl. Al barely so much as touches me. Just a few times. Nothing too forward. The hug just now—I did that. He was drunk, and I was there . . . I shouldn't count it. Anyway, he's married. It's so stupid to imagine there's anything there. I just can't help myself when I'm around him.

All the twisted, crazy scandals in the news—that's other people. Al is Al, and I am me. It would be different.

Even if it wasn't, I don't think I'd mind being one of those girls.

JENNICA

When I come back to Brick's bedroom window, the little guy, Tyrell, is sitting on the ledge, gazing out, the same way I like to. His eyes stream with tears, and he's staring straight through them like he may or may not have noticed them at all. He holds a cup in his hand that's empty except for a drying ring of beer foam.

I lay my hand on his shoulder. "You okay?"

"Is this where I'm supposed to be?" he says. "It feels like I'm supposed to. It feels . . ." He cups his heart with clawed fingers.

"That's the pot talking," I promise him. "You'll be okay."

"I don't think it'll ever be okay."

He's like a little boy looking for guidance or advice. He's looking in the wrong direction.

"I'm not brave," he says. "I can't . . . I don't even like kitchen knives. How'm I gonna—"

I laugh. "You've never gotten high before, have you?"

"No," he says, wiping his nose on his sleeve. "I don't do any drugs."

A surge of anger rises in me. I glance across the room at Brick and Noodle, holding court on the sofas, with crowds of people fawning around. Everything is how they want it. Nothing can be left alone.

"You can just leave," I tell Tyrell. "You don't have to do what Brick says. I know he acts all that, but he's not a bad guy underneath." Strangely, I actually mean it.

"I'm scared to go against him," Tyrell says.

"So how about you walk me home," I tell him. When I see how broken down he seems, it makes me feel stronger. It makes me think I can do anything. Walk away from Noodle, even—if only for tonight. "Then, if he asks you later, you can say you went home with a girl, and he'll give you props."

"You'd do that?" he says. The little-boy eyes perk up.

"Sure."

His face falls. "I can't take Noodle's girl home."

"Just tell Brick it was some girl and you didn't catch her name."

Tyrell shrugs. "Okay."

"Anyway, I'm going to break up with Noodle," I tell Tyrell, as we're headed for the door. Just to try it out. See how it feels. "So for now, I'm really just a girl."

TINA

I know what knives do.
In the kitchen, knives are good.
Chop
Cut
Slice
Dice
Joo-lee-enn, says the cooking lady on TV.
Knives that are not in the kitchen are bad knives.
Stab
Slit
Wound
Fay-tal-i-tee, says the reporter on TV.
Tariq's knife was not in the kitchen.
It is a bad knife.
Bad boys have bad knives.
Tariq was a bad boy, say the voices on TV.
Mommy gets upset.
Nana gets upset.
The Reverend Alabaster Sloan gets upset.
They tell everyone:
Tariq was not a bad boy.

They don't know about the knife.

TYRELL

Grief makes people do crazy things. I read that somewhere. I'm trying not to be too hard on myself. Plus, I'm still a little loopy from the beer and pot at Brick's.

The piece of paper that's taped inside my bedroom closet right now? The chart? I'm gonna blame it on grief. Grief and drunkenness. I'm not a bad person.

Filling out the chart is easy enough. The hard part is the research to make it mean something.

I've always been a numbers guy. It's what I do. I can fix anyone's math homework with a glance. I mean, I try to help them do it themselves because it's better that way. I got a job down at the community center now, three days a week. Tutoring little kids in math. It's good, because I need money, and I need someplace to go after school where no 8-5s are likely to come knocking. But the point is, numbers are what I understand. They make me feel good.

So I make the chart. I pull statistical analyses from online. I know how to identify reputable sources, but it takes some time. In the first column, I write down every name I can think of. Tariq. Sammy. Junior. Brick. Noodle. Guys from school. Guys from church. Guys from the block. The larger the sample size, the better.

The next four columns are topped like this: *Joined a gang. Got locked up. Dropped out. Got killed.* Then I fill in all the Xs. My own statistical analysis. Low level, and not very scientific, but that's what makes it crazy.

I'm not rooting for bad things to happen to people I know. Those things already happened. But the numbers prove . . . the numbers let me believe, at least, that it's all less likely to happen to me.

15. HELPFUL PEOPLE

DAY SEVEN

REVEREND ALABASTER SLOAN

I'm exhausted, hungover, and ready to be done with Tariq Johnson. The first is inevitable. The second, my fault entirely. The third grinds guilt deep into my gut. I'm the one who brought Tariq into the national spotlight. I have to see it through.

I put on a semi-neutral, semi-angry expression as I'm introduced to the country by the grinning host of yet another eponymous news hour. I nod as he offers a slightly inaccurate characterization of the police department's accusation of biased press coverage.

He asks me, "Franklin was released by the police department. Is it right that he's now being tried and convicted by the media?"

"Jack Franklin is not being tried by the media. He can't be.

That's a job for a court and a jury. The media is simply asking questions that law enforcement should be asking."

"Are you saying the police mishandled the investigation?" He grins at me from a monitor mounted beside the camera. Viewers are probably seeing us side-by-side, while I'm in Underhill and he's someplace like Atlanta or New York.

"The police accepted Franklin's narrative," I explain. "By what logic do you accept the shooter's narrative without investigation, especially when there are so many contradictory reports? Why can they take Jack Franklin's word, but not the word of anyone else present?"

"Are you suggesting race bias?"

I fight the urge to sigh, trying instead to channel the fire for which I'm known, beloved, and criticized. "I'm suggesting there be a real investigation. If this case went into a court of law tomorrow, there's absolutely no evidence to back up the story Jack Franklin is telling. And where is Jack Franklin? Law-abiding citizens don't go into hiding."

The host consults his notes. "A spokesman for Franklin says he's keeping a low profile due to press harassment and unfounded accusations."

"Accusations are being leveled both ways," I answer. "Tariq's family isn't hiding. And accusations aren't evidence. Where are the courts in this picture?"

That's all we have time for. The host thanks me for coming, and as the lights dim, I wonder, yet again, what good all these sound bites actually do. They'll be quoted, parsed, fact-checked, eviscerated by those who disagree, and then forgotten in the wake of new blurbs that come out tomorrow.

Tariq will still be dead.

Franklin will still be armed.

Maybe my whole life has been spent pissing into the ocean, trying to turn it yellow.

TYRELL

The school nurse has a flyer taped up on the back of her door about some hoodie march they're planning for Tariq. There's no escaping this thing.

I lie on the black rubber cot and close my eyes, trying to stave off the nausea. Smoking and drinking don't agree with me, apparently. I had already figured as much, but now I know for sure. I roll toward the plastic-lined waste bin and heave.

Last time I got sick at school, two years ago, it was some kind of flu bug going around. I caught it in the middle of Spanish class, fourth period. Right after lunch. It was pretty epically disgusting. I felt it coming on, a kind of low volcanic rumbling in my stomach, and I tried to run for it, but only made it as far as the classroom doorway before I blew chunks of Salisbury steak and broccoli all over the tile.

The whole class went, "Awww, man!" 'cause it was so nasty. It was too embarrassing to even look back, so I just kept on running till I got to the nurse's office. She took one glance at the mess on my shirt and said, "You can go home."

You're supposed to have a parent come pick you up when something like that happens, but I live only ten blocks from school, and I told the nurse my mom was out of town and my dad was at work. She knew I was a good student, so she gave me a clean T-shirt and just let me walk home, sparing me the humiliation of going back to class and having to stare at a pile of sawdust soaking up my stomach contents.

I trudged home, feeling pretty lousy, only to discover something worse.

Four feet in the bed, and Mom out of town.

"God damn it, Tyrell," Dad bellowed. "What are you doing home?"

I opened my mouth to say "I'm sick," but it came out as another burst of vomit. Dad might have misinterpreted it.

"Clean that up," Dad snapped. "And keep your mouth shut." He slammed the bedroom door in my face.

So I took rags and a spray bottle from the cupboard, got down on my knees, and scrubbed away all signs of my sickness, to the soundtrack of Dad and his . . . friend . . . huffing and puffing on the other side of the door.

Mom always took care of me when I got sick. Dad wouldn't know the thing to do for a fever and flu was to hold a cool washcloth on my forehead, and rub my hands real soft, and give me crackers, and let me watch DVDs of vintage *Star Trek* on the sofa. So I stayed in my room.

I kept waiting for Dad to come in and say "It wasn't what you think" or "I can explain."

But he never even knocked. After a while, everything went quiet. Later I heard the TV go on in the living room. He didn't want anything to do with me.

That hasn't changed.

"You can probably get anything you want now," T said, when I told him what had happened with my dad. It was a long time after, almost a year. At the point when things had gotten so bad I could barely stand to be in the house with Dad just hating me all over the place. Mom knew something was going on, but what was I going to say?

"What do you mean?"

"From your dad. You have this information that he doesn't want out there. You can use that to your advantage."

"No, I can't."

I can't do anything but feel shame when Dad looks at me. Maybe if I was more manly, like he wants me to be, I would have reacted differently. Maybe I wouldn't feel like crap every time Mom says, "What's troubling you?" and I say, "Nothing." Maybe I could just roll with it. If I was the right kind of son.

I don't fit in at home. I don't fit in out on the street. Only place I ever fit was with T. Thinking about it only makes me miss him more.

The nurse sends me back to class, but I find myself walking right out of the building. I can't stay at school. I can't go home, either. My head pounds, and I feel kinda full and kinda hungry at the same time. My guts are churning.

Tariq's been gone seven days. That's a whole week. Last thing we did together was make our can-collection rounds. That means it's time again. It's a scheme we came up with to help earn some spending money. Although, I mostly saved mine. Brick was right about that much—applying to college isn't cheap, let alone actually going. But I can't afford to put aside my schoolwork to get a normal job. Tutoring pays peanuts, but it's easy. I can do my homework at the same time, and it'll look real good for my transcripts.

The city comes by and collects cans. Some homeless guys go through trash bins on the street and sort through people's recycling from the curb to get bottles to turn in. Five cents each. It's a real commitment if you're trying to make serious dough. Tariq had the genius idea that if we talked to some neighbors and got them to hold their cans and bottles for us, we wouldn't have to rummage and it'd be guaranteed cash.

We'd hit one block at a time, me going down one side and T going down the other. I'll have to do both sides of the street myself now, I guess. And get double the money too. I try to let that make me happy.

I go down the block on my regular side, knocking. Someone usually opens the door. Soon I'm dragging a few plastic sacks down Peach Street. Past the place where it happened and the brick wall that now bears Tariq's face. *Miss you, buddy.*

I knock. The door opens. "Hi, Mr. Arlen. You got any cans for me?"

"Hi, Tyrell." He leaves the door half open and walks out of sight to wherever he keeps his recycling. He's a white guy, and he likes his beer. He usually gives us a decent haul. "Yeah, I got a big load for you this week." He reappears with a bulging sack of cans and bottles.

From the background comes the rubber-sucking, jar-rattling sound of a fridge door opening.

"Oh, sorry," I tell him. "I didn't mean to bother you while you had company."

"Don't worry about it," he says, his voice growing tense.

A shadow moves across the hallway behind him. My eye goes to it automatically. I see a face that I've seen every day on television. A face that now looms in my nightmares.

EDWIN "ROCKY" FRY

Tyrell brings in cans to recycle. He has a troubled look in his eye. On account of how he used to bring in cans with Tariq, I figure. They made decent money at it.

"How are you holding up?" I ask him.

"I'm okay," he says, real clipped. He's here to do business, not chitchat. I can respect that. I won't even ask him what he's doing out of school.

"Do you want cash, or do you want to buy anything?"

He places several wrapped snack cakes on the counter. "And some cigarettes," he says. "Maybe three packs?"

I frown. "I'm pretty sure you're underage. Am I wrong?"

Tyrell hesitates. "I really need them," he says. I give him credit for that. Most guys would lie. They come in trying all the time, even ones I've known since they were little.

"You smoke now?"

"No, sir." He looks properly disgusted at the thought. Hmm.

"Please," he adds. "It's important."

I don't break the law for anyone. But how can I not take pity on those sad eyes? "Well," I tell him, "I can't sell you cigarettes, but I can pay you a dollar to deliver some for me." I pull three packs off the shelf. Lay them on the counter with a dollar.

"Deliver them where?" Tyrell asks.

"Well, I can't rightly remember the address." I put a pen and slip of paper on the counter. "Maybe you can help me out."

Tyrell's a smart kid. He takes my pen and writes down an address. I assume it's his own.

"So, you leave me your money, and on the other end, you collect it back. So we'll be square, and you don't have to make two trips."

"I understand. Thank you."

I bag up the cigs and cakes for him. And he skitters out of there like a scared rabbit.

JENNICA

Noodle calls, and I let it go to voice mail. Time and time again. I hold the phone in my hand as it vibrates relentlessly.

Eventually I set it aside on the edge of my bed and lie there contemplating it. The main thoughts that flash through my mind have to do with the first time I ever saw Noodle. The memory still makes me flush warm.

It's natural, in the end, to get nostalgic about the beginning. Isn't it?

The diner was real busy that day, and it wasn't too long after I started working there. I had the counter, plus a bunch of tables of two and one table of four. I know now the four-top was Tariq and Brick, with their sisters. At the time, they were just two guys I'd never laid eyes on before. I'd probably seen them around, I'm sure, but not to recognize or call by name.

I remember thinking they were real sweet, being all goofy with the girls, who were charming. I spent more time than I should have lingering by their table. I can't remember anything about what they ate, but I'm sure that taking his order that day was the longest exchange of words I ever had with Tariq, direct. I almost sort of forgot about it until now.

A half hour after they'd left, Noodle breezed in, looking for Brick.

"Hey," he said, his gaze running up and down me. "You're looking good." In that low, sexy drawl guys use when they're flirting.

"Everyone looks good in a uniform," I snapped. To be honest, I wasn't in the mood. I had a lot of tables to cover.

"Naw," he says. "That's just what they want you to believe."

He bent in close, so close it stole my breath. He was beautiful to me. Tall and lean and *interested*. I thought he was going to kiss me. "Coffee to go," he said, his breath fanning my cheek. "I'll be back for something else."

And he did come back. And I liked him. I didn't know everything then, about how the Kings would become his whole life. I just fell for him.

All of that was almost two years ago. Two years of his breath on my cheek. Two years of "something else."

Noodle doesn't stop calling. The phone shakes and buzzes on the edge of my mattress for an eternity. The square little picture of him blinks at me, and when it finally fades, I'm relieved.

REDEEMA

Them heavy fists at the door. I can hardly pull myself to answer it, so wary and weary I've become. I barely crack it open 'fore they push me out the way. Thunder past me like a blue streak. A dozen uniformed cops. "Ma'am, we have a warrant to search the premises for evidence of drugs or other illegal activity on the part of Tariq Johnson."

Two of them pen us in the corner of the kitchen. Thrust thick sheaves of paper in my face. I snatch them, try to read it as if I understand the law-talk, which I might, if the print were big enough to make out. My reading glasses are on the coffee table, and ain't none of these pigs willing to go fetch 'em for me.

Tina darts between them and runs to her room to hide. Under the bed, no doubt. They let her go. I don't like her being alone back there, with so many strange men in the house, but they stop me trying to go to her.

Vernie can barely stand for the outrage. "You've got no right!" she screams. "My son is the victim here."

They come out of Tariq's room waving a bunch of cash in an evidence bag. "There's more than a hundred dollars here. You give your son that kind of allowance?"

Cop looks around the apartment. Under a stranger's eye, I know it won't look so good. Walls in need of paint. Chipped tile. Linoleum all buckled and faded. A crack in the window, covered over with tape. We get by. We save our money for what matters.

Cop sniffs rudely. "No, I reckon he couldn't have come by this much cash honestly."

They confiscate it. DRUG MONEY? gets written on the bag. I watch them scrawl it in thick black marker, right on our own kitchen counter. They open every cabinet. Sniff our flour, our sugar, each spice. Drag all the frozen food out of the freezer. We'll have to replace damn near everything.

Vernie is incoherent, screaming. I hold her tight. Hold her back, so she don't do nothing we're all gonna regret.

I take Vernie's cell phone out of her housecoat pocket, dial the Reverend Sloan. "You best get over here. And bring some of them cameras."

VERNESHA

"No, they didn't find anything," I tell the Reverend Sloan. "I don't even know what they were looking for."

My entire body is quaking. I don't know how to loosen the knots of rage and pain. *Will I have to live like this?* After the funeral, I'd thought there could be no deeper low. I want to think it again now, but I have been stripped of all certainty.

"Probably some kind of evidence they could use to vilify Tariq," Sloan says.

Mom serves us tea on her most delicate china. Not the everyday mugs. I wonder at that, but I can't find the will to really care. Sloan has seen all the crappy corners of our life already. What does it matter?

"This will be small comfort," Sloan adds, "but there was a camera crew on-site when they arrived. Additional media arrived in time to catch footage of the police leaving the building. People will be outraged on your behalf."

Outraged? My ears ring. They don't begin to know.

TINA

Out my window, red and blue lights flash.
In my room, the policemen move my things.
The clothes I wear.
The fuzzy rabbit Tariq gave me.
The books we like to read.
I pick up the book called *Helpful People*.
I like this book, especially the pictures.
And how Tariq always does funny voices when he reads it.
When I go outside, sometimes I look for helpful people.
Doctors and nurses and firemen and teachers,
Lawyers and mail carriers and mommies and daddies.
Page four says
Policemen solve problems and help keep you safe.
Policemen are always on your side.
I tear out page four and crumple it into a ball.
Page three comes with it, which is sad,
But there is nothing I can do.

TYRELL

It's a long bus ride to the state prison. Three hours one way. I don't know how people do this on the regular.

I checked the visiting hours online. I know I should make it in plenty of time. It's going to take the rest of the day, and it's just as well. Out of school, can't go home, can't wander the neighborhood without running into someone I don't want to see.

I do my math homework on the bus, but it doesn't take three hours. So after that I just look out the window. Nothing to see, really. Outside the city, there are houses for a while, but then it turns into wide flat land on either side of a road that goes into infinity.

JUNIOR

"Collins, you got a visitor." Guard pounds on my bars, shaking me out of my nap.

"Me?" I try not to look too surprised.

"Said your name, didn't I? Let's go."

"All right." I roll up off the cot and follow him down the hallway.

I never get visitors. My moms doesn't even come up here anymore. It got to be too much. She means well, but I could tell it was hurting her back to be on that long bus ride. Not to mention the cost. She came once a week for the first month. Then every other for two months. Then down to once a month for the next three, until finally I just told her, don't worry about it. I'm not going anywhere. She says she's coming up on my birthday, but that's still a month away.

I can't think of anybody else who'd want to see me.

The guard leads me through the maze of security doors to the visitation room. "Number four," he says.

I move down the row to the fourth cubicle. Sitting on the other side of the glass is, well, just about the last person I would've expected to see.

I pick up the bright orange phone. "What are you doing here, Ty?"

"Hey, Junior," he says. "I—I don't know."

I look at him. He looks thin. Scared. Guy like him, seeing a place like this? "Long way to travel for 'I don't know.'"

"Yeah." His fingers squeeze the phone coil. He looks at me.

The folding chair creaks as I lean back, settle in. "You know they don't give me all day up in here."

"Right. Um, how are you?"

"I'm locked up. How you think I am?"

Ty licks his lips. "Sorry."

It's out of place to be mad at him. He's come all this way. But it ain't to see me. Can't be. Ten months, not one friend been by. So-called friends. So-called brothers.

"You bring me anything?"

"Yeah," he says. "Some cigarettes and some cakes from Rocky's. I think I remember the ones. I didn't know what—" He swallows. "Anyway, they took it when I got here."

"I'll get it back," I tell him. "They think they gotta check it first. They don't know what a do-gooding kinda punk you are."

Ty smiles. There we go. Like old times.

I decide to give him a break. "That's nice, man. Thanks."

"You doing okay?" he says. "For real?"

"Look around," I tell him. "What do you want me to say?"

He glances around kind of loosely. The walls, the glass, the guards. The fact that we can't even slap skin after not seeing each other for better than a year, when we used to be so close we shared a sleeping bag.

"You heard about Tariq?" he asks.

Figures it would be something to do with that. "Yeah. Bad rap."

"I thought maybe you wouldn't find out."

"You came all the way up here to tell me that? It's been in the news."

"I—"

"They're saying he oathed in," I say. "I thought you guys were sticking it together on the outside."

"I thought so, too," Ty says, so quiet the orange phone garbles his voice.

He touches the finger-stained glass. "I hate that you're in here, man." It comes from someplace deep in his throat. I feel the meaning of it. "I can't believe—"

"You always was the softie," I say. My own voice scratches. "You stay true, okay, bro?"

"I don't know," he says.

Now we're getting to it. Like a light switching on, I know why he's here.

I lean forward. "Listen to me, man."

He's listening.

"You be you. No matter what. Who's dogging you—Brick?"

Ty clutches the phone.

"Look," I tell him, "I'm supposed to say all kinds of things about what the Kings can do for you. What they did for me. And they still got my back in here, so I ain't got a bad thing to say about them, okay?" I pull at my jumpsuit. "But this is what they did for me, you know?"

"Do you wish, I mean, if you had it to do over—"

"Don't go there, man." Thinking like that will drive you crazy on the inside. "I ain't have any other choice. I did what I had to." I glance around, though we're in a soundproof booth.

"I'm in here because of Sciss," I whisper.

"I know that," Ty says.

"Do you?" Maybe Tariq told him.

He nods. "I read your trial transcript. Things didn't add up."

That sounds like Ty. Always doing the math.

He looks like he's going to cry. If I could reach through the glass, I would put my hand on his shoulder. Nothing to lose for me in it now. Ty was always Ty. Too soft for the street. Too soft for this life. We'd have to break him. Harden him. For the first time, for a moment, I'm grateful to be on the inside. If that's what has to happen, watching it would be too much to bear.

"Stay strong, bro. You always was the strongest of us. Don't let them get you. You hear me?"

"What can I do?" he says. "I don't have any friends left."

"Friends let you down, man. You gotta just do what you do."

"Time," the guard says. "Wrap it up."

"T never let me down," Tyrell says. Me either. He's still got my knife, ain't he? I wonder what'll happen to it now.

The guard's standing over me now. In a second, they'll cut off the phone line. In the last breath before dead air, I tell Ty the truth. "T woulda said the same about you. Even if he went down, he wouldn't want that for you."

TYRELL

I thought we'd have more time. I meant to ask Junior what I should do about the Franklin situation. I laid eyes on him, cold and clear, in the back of Tom Arlen's house.

Brick wants to go after him. I heard him talking about it with Noodle the other night. Information is power. I just don't know how to use it.

I had to go see Junior. It helps to catch a glimpse of the end-game. Join the Kings, break the law, end up behind bars. No question. Most of the Kings do some kind of time. Brick himself was inside for a year not that long ago. *It's the life,* T would say. *That's why we don't want any part of it.*

Junior was trying to tell me something in the end there, before they cut him off and took him back to lockup. I could see the intensity in his eyes; all I heard was "he went down," and then static.

I'm ashamed of the rush I got hearing that. Maybe it's time I admit it. All along, some part of me was rooting for T to go down just so I could stay afloat.

Seventy-five percent of black men in Underhill join up. If Tariq was in, then it gives me that much more chance to stay out. If Tariq wasn't, then he's still the guy I thought he was, but it makes it that much more likely that I'm gonna cave, now that he's gone.

TINA

The policemen took away a lot of Tariq's things,
But they did not find the big red knife.
I am good at hiding things.
Tariq's bad knife lives in my room now.
I can't forget that it is there,
But I can remember not to touch it anymore.
It was only a mistake, the first time.
Tariq says if I find something dangerous,
Don't touch it.
Just tell him.
I will always protect you, Tariq promised.
I can keep promises, too.

16. DEATH SHROUD
DAY EIGHT

KIMBERLY

As I'm hurrying back toward Mollie's, I see Jennica. She steps out the door of the salon, shoulders slumped. But her face brightens when she sees me coming.

"Hi." She's wearing a hooded sweatshirt. "I was looking for you. They told me you weren't working today."

"I'm not. I came to drop these off"—I raise the bags in my arms—"and put on my hoodie."

"You headed down to the march?" Along Peach Street here, small knots of hooded people roll toward Roosevelt Park.

"Yeah." I hike the heavy bags up on my shoulder. She's lingering, though, waiting as if she has more to say. "You okay?"

She shifts her sandaled feet, flicking the toe of one sandal with the toe of the other. "This is weird, but do you want to go down together, maybe?" she says.

"I'm working with Reverend Sloan," I tell her. "I have some responsibilities at the march."

"Oh." She looks smaller now, disappointed.

"You don't want to go with your boyfriend?" I've seen her around enough to know she hangs with Brick's close guy. Noodle. I don't want to get anywhere near that mess.

"I don't think they're going," she says. "And I don't want to go by myself."

"All right, then."

Jennica perks up. I feel good about that. These past few days with Al have shown me that sometimes all a person needs is a little jolt of support to feel more confident. I'm used to going places by myself, but I can see why it would make someone like her feel weird.

"I mean, it might be kind of boring, but you can come along with me." It's not like I'm going up on stage with him.

"How did you do it?" Jennica blurts.

"Do what?" I ask.

"Stay away from the Kings."

She seems real serious, so I hold back my laugh. "They never wanted me," I answer. Why would they?

"I want a different kind of life," Jennica says. Everything she says comes out like she thinks it shouldn't be said.

"Who doesn't?" I answer. My perfect little DC apartment is alive and well in my mind.

TINA

Hoodie
Hoodie
Mommy says
Put on your hoodie
I don't like things
covering my head

Hoodie
Hoodie
Mommy says
To honor Tariq
No
No hoodie

Mommy says
Do it for Tariq
But
Tariq would not have made me

NOODLE

My hoodie that's clean is the one that's a little tight. But I ain't doing laundry. Not for Tariq.

It's bad enough that Brick's ordering us all to go to this whacked-out march in the first place. Now I have to dress for it.

Tariq gets a vigil. Tariq gets a march. Can't turn on the TV without hearing the latest in the Tariq Johnson case. Can't get away from it.

I'm watching the coverage now, pretty regular. I've seen myself on TV a couple of times. I keep hoping to catch another glimpse. It was exciting for a while, being in it, but it's getting old.

The news is acting like Tariq was the first kid ever shot in Underhill. Well, he wasn't. We've lost Kings before. We've put plenty of pain on the Stingers too. No one looks twice.

I don't see the point. Tariq isn't worth all this fuss. Ain't a damn thing special about him.

STEVE CONNERS

I catch Will heading out the door, wearing a hoodie. "I thought your mom took those away."

"Get off my back," he snaps at me.

"I hope you're not thinking of going down to that protest."

"So what if I am?"

"I know they're trying to make it a race-relations issue on TV. I'm proud of you for wanting to support that, but it's a bad neighborhood."

"Bad 'cause it's where the black people live?"

"Not all black people."

He smirks at me. "Riiiiight."

Everything I say is coming out wrong. "It's about more than race—" I try.

Will smirks harder. "You got shelves and shelves of history books, Steve. Sociology. Race and politics. How come you still think racism's in the past?" I'm vaguely surprised he knows what's on my shelves. He's never shown much interest in my library. He yo-yos between the kitchen and his bedroom, and that's about it.

"Do you read my books?" I ask him.

"What, now that's off limits too?"

"I didn't mean that. I meant—I didn't know you were interested in reading."

"You think I can't read now?"

"You're putting words in my mouth."

"You're taking them out of mine."

It's heated between us. It never has been. This is new ground. Best to stand firm. "You can't go down there."

"I know guys like Tariq," Will says. "I got a right to go down there."

"Not anymore."

"You saying I got no rights?"

"He was a low-life gang member. That's most likely, isn't it?" I don't like saying it. Not sure I mean it, but there it is.

"What if he wasn't?" Will shouts. His hands tremble as he throws down his backpack. "What if I still lived down there? I like fucking Snickers."

I don't know why he has to use this gutter language, but I swallow any scolding words. Because I hear him. For the first time, I hear it, so loud and so strong. I hear him saying, *This could happen to me.*

WILL (AKA eMZee)

"I'm not going to let anything happen to you," Steve says, in response to my shouting. He steps up as if to take me by the shoulders, but I break free and race off to my room. It's not up to him, is it? I can go out the window, like always. Instead I lie on my bed and stare at the ceiling.

I don't hear Steve coming; when I happen to glance over at the doorway, he's standing there silently, looking at me. I don't know for how long.

"Will you loan me a hoodie?" Steve says. Now, after all that, he wants to go with me to the march.

"Mom took them, remember?" I answer, thrusting the words at him. "This one isn't even mine." I glare at him, glad for once to show my defiance. He has to know—I can't be held down by his rules, his world.

"Let's find them," he says. His voice sounds gruff.

Steve drives us, which takes much less time than the bus. He pays for parking in a crowded garage. I should have made him come to Underhill my way. Show him how the other half lives. Not that he could ever understand.

We head out of the garage, but I find myself turning the opposite direction from the park. Steve follows.

"I want to show you around the neighborhood first," I tell him, which comes as a surprise to both of us.

"All right."

We walk past our old apartment and my former schools. I point out some street murals I like, but I don't mention I painted them. I show him the diner where Mom and I used to go all the time. Steve buys us milkshakes to go and we keep walking.

It's crowded at the park, where people have begun to gather. It's not quite sundown, but there's clearly going to be a big turn-out. We are folded in among them, and we look up at the stage, with all the speakers and microphones. The Reverend Sloan is up there, and Tariq's mom, grandma, and little sister holding hands. The speeches start and finish, and then the march begins. We parade through the streets of Underhill, past the site of the shooting, making our way toward police headquarters and City Hall downtown.

Steve puts his arm around my shoulders. If he has ever touched me before today, I can't remember it. I don't shrug away. It doesn't have to mean anything, I realize. It's just the feeling of the crowd, so easy to get caught up in. Among all the candles and the hoodies and the low, eerie chant: *Justice for Tariq. We want justice for Tariq.*

Steve squeezes my shoulder. I look up at him and his mouth is moving, along with the chant. His cheeks are streaked with tears.

My chest fills with a burst of feeling, unlike anything I've ever experienced before. I never knew my real dad. Mom says he wasn't a fatherly type of guy, which always seemed like an obvious thing to say, since he wasn't around. Steve's arm tightens around me, and my eyes start going too. He doesn't say a word, but I just know, the way you know things sometimes. I am under his wing, and I am in his heart.

I won't try to be your father, he told me, the day we moved our things into his house. I was grateful for him saying it, from that minute to this one, but I wonder now. Maybe that plan can't last.

TOM ARLEN

I keep the curtains closed, but for a slit. So I can see out. Crowds gather slowly through the late afternoon, clad in hoodies, carrying posters and hand-painted signs.

Peach Street no longer streams with the quiet flow of the vigil. Voices now ring with whitewater fury; the air itself turns angry and intense and it pushes through the walls and sends my houseguest to the liquor cabinet again and again.

"They're going to get me," he says. "I should have left town."

"You're all right," I tell him, though I'm sure it's a lie. I don't know what Tyrell saw, or who he'll tell.

Tyrell's a good kid, though. Real responsible. Comes for my recycling every week, like clockwork, all on his own initiative. He's saving for college, he told me. I highly doubt he hangs around with the likes of Tariq Johnson and the Kings.

I reassure Jack again. "No one's trying to get you."

Through the crack in the curtains it all seems less certain. We just sit and we drink and try not to listen.

JENNICA

"Okay, ready," Kimberly says, popping back onto the sidewalk in jeans and a green hoodie. She carries a sleek black folder of papers and a cell phone in her hand, clicking away with her thumbs. I feel like I'm really intruding on her now, but I guess I'm desperate. I need her. There has to be someone, and without Noodle there's no one, and it's like a free fall that hasn't started yet but it's about to, and maybe I will crash and maybe I'll die, or maybe I'll get lucky and find somewhere else to land, away from him. If I can be like Kimberly, so beautiful and strong, maybe it won't hurt so bad if all that happens at the end of the fall is that I crash into the earth.

"I'm sorry," I tell her. "Thanks for letting me come along."

"That's okay," she says. "Maybe it'll be fun." I suppose it's a weird thing to say about an event like this, but I know what she means.

I don't know if we're exactly friends or what, or if she's taking pity on me, or how pathetic I must seem to her, being tethered to Noodle like I have been. He's called three times in the past half hour, and I just let it ring and ring.

"Are you ignoring him?" Kimberly asks.

"Maybe," I admit.

It's buzzing again now. I've turned off the sound, but the vibrations tremble out from my pocket, through my hips and stomach and up and down my limbs. Like a shiver.

Outside in the crowd, Kimberly links arms with me, and I feel stronger. We walk amid the jostle, and the darkening sky fills with sad music. It's not clear who is singing. It isn't us at first, but after a while it is. It's all of us.

The little guy from the other night, Tyrell, weaves through the mobs, alone and hooded. A glimpse of his chin and cheek is all I get as he's passing, but it's enough to recognize. I touch his arm, and he smiles at me. We link arms too; a lot of people are linked, and there's strength in that, there's a river of hope in that.

There is a podium stage in the park, and the Reverend Sloan is on it. Kimberly sucks in her breath when he starts to speak. We're on the fringes of things, and I don't want to get any closer. I thought that to face this thing would help purge it, but each moment only pushes Tariq deeper into me. The flit of his hand on my skin or the taste of his breath in the air—it must have been his last breath that I tasted, I grow more and more certain—and it's a part of my every breath, and maybe that's how it'll always be. Maybe I can learn to breathe around it.

"Shh," Kimberly says. "You're okay. We're okay."

I've been stuck for a while in a place without tears. Not any-more. The swelling music, the soft hoodie, the linked arms bol-stering me. It's all too much.

"Shh," she says.

"Oh, God," Tyrell breathes. His arm snakes out of the loop in mine.

With my newly freed hand, I push back my hood to find Noodle steaming toward me.

NOODLE

Bitch has been ignoring my calls. I storm up to her. "What gives?"

"I thought you weren't coming," she says. Her face is a mess of tears. I'm getting tired of all this.

"So you thought you'd come without me?" I grab her and yank her away from the big girl she's linked up with.

"Hey," says the other girl.

"What are you doing here?" Jennica cries. "Let go."

"Brick changed his mind. If you picked up your phone, you might know that."

"You didn't leave any messages," she says.

"You could have just picked up."

"Maybe I couldn't."

She always has before. No matter when I call. She makes time for me.

"First you leave without a word last night and then you're not picking up and now you're down here with this chickenshit punk?" Tyrell is small and getting smaller, backing away. "What gives?" I say again.

"I want to break up," she says. "I can't be with you anymore. We're breaking up." She throws the words at me. Like a fistfight, one punch after the other.

I just look at her. The tears are ugly, but she is still beautiful, and there is no way I'm letting her go. My fists clench around her biceps, tight and tighter, until she turns her head away and the cries become cries of pain.

"No," I say. It won't happen this way. I won't let it. "No."

"You can't say no," she tells me. "It's done."

JENNICA

My arms sting from the insistence in Noodle's grip, and I don't know how many times I have to say it. *It's done. We're done. Let me go.*

"That hurts," I tell him finally, which I've never been able to tell him before, and I don't know if it's the way the people around us have pushed back their hoodies to look at us locked together or how everything's out in the open.

He relaxes his fists.

"I didn't mean to do this in front of people," I admit. "I'm sorry." The people around us are strangers, except for Brick, who's coming up now, and Kimberly and Tyrell, who are standing there helpless.

Noodle drags me to the edge of the crowd, away from his friends and mine. The rest of the people flow past, indifferent to everything but Tariq.

I'm already drained to empty, but Noodle's in front of me, and even though it's over between us, the part where it actually *becomes* over isn't finished. Not yet.

The hollow feeling in my gut isn't hunger.

I don't expect anything to change, really. I'll get up in the morning, go to school, go to work. Quieter evenings, I guess. Just by myself at home. No Noodle. No girlfriends, because they all hook up with Kings and hang at King parties. But I won't.

I don't know who I'll hang out with exactly. Kimberly, maybe, if tonight hasn't made her think I'm a total spaz loser and scared her away. Auntie Anjelica will worry if I stop going out altogether, but I can't think about that now.

"No one leaves a King," Noodle thunders at me.

"You leave me, then," I say. "I don't care how you tell it."

"Who is it?" he says. "There's some other guy?"

"There's no one. This is just what I want."

I'm crying worse now. It's been almost two years. I've seen every kind of face he has to offer. Seen him mad. Seen him tender. Seen him sexy. Seen him puffed up. Seen him laughing. Seen him high.

Never seen him cry. Never heard "I'm sorry."

Still don't.

BRICK

Noodle comes back to us heated. "That bitch," he says. "I'm better off."

"What happened?"

"I cut her loose," he goes.

I raise my brow. "Yeah?" They were together a long time.

"Shit," Noodle says. "She's acting the fool. This Tariq thing screwed with her mind. I ain't got time for that crap."

"Sure, sure." I crane my neck and look through the crowd, try to see after her. I want— I don't know. I want to let her know she can still come around my place. I'll keep Noodle off if that's the deal. Jennica's the best girl we hang with. It'd suck to lose her. How could you not want that in front of you? That smile. Those eyes. Let alone the rest of her.

Noodle pounds a fist into his palm. "I wanna fuck someone up," he goes. His eye falls on Tyrell. "You," he goes, pointing. "What do you think you're doing, hanging with my girl?"

"Hey, hey." I nudge Noodle off, because it looks like he's about to jump the poor little guy, and if there was ever a recruitment killer, it's getting your face beat to a pulp by a so-called friend. "Ty's okay. And she's not your girl now, anyway," I remind him. "You said so."

"Chickenshit punk," he spits, glaring at Tyrell over my shoulder. "You think you got what it takes? You think you wanna be a King? You ain't got nothing!"

Noodle postures up against me, making for Tyrell. I push him off. "Fucking chill," I order him. But he can't and I can't blame him, because I walk around with my eyes open, which means I saw it coming, and it means I know he lied, and nothing's worse than when your girl walks off and ends it. That's if you love her, and he does.

"*Fuck*," he screams, in a rage against the sky. The hooded people turn and stare, in a wave, like a thousand grim reapers. This march is much too morbid, I realize, everyone clad in Tariq's death shroud. Noodle's fury is more right, more real. Losing Jennica rips him. Losing Tariq rips me even deeper. Because it's definitely forever.

I could lay Noodle out in a second. But I don't. My mind works smooth, which is why I'm in charge. Instead I tighten my arms around his chest. It ain't gangster, but it's necessary.

"There's a lot of cameras here," I whisper. "Let's take a walk." It's a peaceful protest. Can't go calling attention to ourselves like this.

Tyrell steps up behind me. I feel him move in close. Think to myself, *Maybe he's got stones after all*. By now I'd have figured he'd be long gone and running.

He speaks quiet enough for my ears and Noodle's alone. The fury that's over all of us reflected in his voice. Not heated and flailing. Cold as ice.

"What?" I demand, not believing what I just heard him say.

"You wanna fuck someone up?" Tyrell says again. "How about Jack Franklin? I know where he is."

TYRELL

Amid the surge of everything, Brick and Noodle whisk me out of the crowd, around the corner, and down the alley behind Rocky's store. Sammy's with us too. I breathe a sigh to be out of the masses, but it is not a sigh of relief. There is no relief for anything I feel.

"You know where Franklin is?" Noodle asks. It's just the four of us now, in the relative quiet. There is still the cobwebbing music from beyond and now also a musty cardboard stench in the alley and the frequent whiff of garbage.

I nod. It was rash, what I said. It just came out of me under the pressure of the moment. And there's no taking it back. "He's right here. In Underhill."

"That's too easy," Noodle hoots. "Idiot. What's he doing down here?"

"Asking for it," Sammy says.

"Straight up," Brick says. "We'll give it to him."

"Just tell us where," Noodle says. "We'll go fuck him up together." I'm grateful that the murderous light in his eyes is now directed at someone other than me.

"No," Brick says, which surprises me. "Tyrell found him. Tyrell gets to fuck him up."

They turn to me. Four eyes in two hulking bodies; they put me in a pressure cooker. I glance at Sammy for help, but he's looking straight through me, real intense, with his hand held up around his hip.

"This is your time, Tyrell." Brick's arm goes around my shoulders, heavy and sure. "You're gonna show Jack Franklin who's boss."

The lid's on, the heat is up, and I can't see a way out. I shake my head anyway. "I—"

Brick draws his knife. "You can use this. After tonight, you'll earn a blade of your own. I got it waiting for you at my place."

"I can't," I whisper.

"Sure you can," Brick says. "All you gotta do is think about how this is the guy that took Tariq away. The guy that fucked up your best friend and got away with it. He's gonna get away with it, Ty. Can't you feel that? You're smart. You watch the news. You know how it's gonna go down."

Brick leans in closer. "Think about his face on the news, and how no one in the goddamn world knows where he is to bring him justice—except you. You and this knife." He arcs it in front of me, slowly, such that I see my reflection in its blade even in the gathering dusk.

It plays out in my mind, as Brick is speaking. Franklin, down and bleeding. Me standing over him. The tight way Brick is pacing—I have that same tightness inside me, looking for a way to get out.

"You want me to kill him?" I gulp. I've heard you have to do something really bad to be initiated. Did Tariq have to kill a guy?

Did he have blood on his hands, like Franklin? I can't imagine it. I'm sure he couldn't. Wouldn't. Didn't.

Noodle laughs, high-pitched and dissonant with the eerie music from the march.

"I think he's gonna die," Brick says. "I think our blades are gonna do it, but not tonight."

"Tonight is just a warning," Noodle says. "Mess with the Kings, you get cut."

That's probably what Sciss told Junior, wasn't it? Just a cut. I shiver, but it doesn't shake away the rush I feel underneath.

"The police aren't coming for him," Brick tells me. "They love a guy like Franklin. Someone down in City Hall's probably making him up a passport right now. He's gonna fly to Buenos Aires and live in paradise forever. So it's up to us to bring him justice. . . ." He draws the knife through the air across my throat, too close for comfort.

"I'll fuck him up," Noodle says, pounding his fist as a demonstration. "Then all you got to do is cut him." He draws a switchblade quick as a flash and slices it through the air in front of me, three short, fast strokes. Down, angle, angle. The shape of a *K*.

Brick extends the knife to me again. "As soon as the crowd breaks up," he says. "You're on."

SAMMY

Brick's forgetting the fact that Tyrell hasn't told us yet where to find Franklin. I'm betting, in the end, he won't. It's written in his eyes how scared he is. I don't think he has the heart to cut a guy.

We go back to Brick's place to wait it out, but the crowds don't break up. The hoodie march has a life of its own, and eventually Noodle is too wasted to fuck anybody up, and though Brick is impatient, it seems like the marchers will be at it until dawn.

Deep inside me, I'm grateful. Ty won't have to cut anybody tonight, and maybe I can get the chance to change things. Maybe Noodle's high will dampen the memory of how enraged and hurt he is, and maybe Brick won't press the issue in the light of day . . . but these are just things I'm telling myself. I want this shot. I deserve it. What has Ty ever done to step up into this place?

When I catch him slipping out the door in the middle of the night, I follow.

"Just let me go, please," he says. "I'm really tired."

"I'm not out here to make you come back in," I promise. "I just wanted to see if you're okay."

He sighs, deflates. "Not really. I can't— I don't know what I was thinking. I'm not even a hundred percent sure of what I know."

He's lying about that, I can tell.

"Look, you can use the information however you want," I tell him, realizing this is the answer to all of my problems.

He brightens. "I've been thinking about trying to make a deal. You think Brick'll leave me alone after this, if I tell him?" he says.

Brick would never go for that.

"You don't have to tell them at all," I suggest. "Why don't you just tell me?"

17. KNIFE

EDWIN "ROCKY" FRY

I did good business last night. More than double my usual sales in the last week, overall. I should be ecstatic, but the headlines still pain me.

10,000 TURN OUT TO MARCH FOR TARIQ

I couldn't keep enough bottled water cold in the fridge. People bought it warm. Snacks flew off the shelf. They marched their hearts out. I'm not sure it did anyone but my cash register any good.

LEGISLATURE VOTES DOWN GUN REFORM BILL

The timing is strange on that one. They had it in committee for months. All the pressure around Tariq brought it forward this week. If they were going to vote it down, why did they even bother? It's like they went out of the way to say, *No, what happened here is fine.*

SLOAN RISES IN POLLS

I guess I wasn't the only one to benefit in a significant way from what's been going on. I have to make peace, somehow, with my place in all of this. Peach Street is still my home; I can't keep thinking of it as a war zone, or a protest platform, or a deathbed. Put one foot in front of the other, go to work. Read the news; sprinkle liberally with salt. Ring up. Make change. Smile. Chitchat.

Thanks. Have a nice day.

KIMBERLY

First thing in the morning, I hurry over to the hotel. I'm practically bouncing with energy after last night's march. To think I helped put it together. Some of the media people I emailed and called actually showed! It was so exciting.

Joy bubbles up through my veins. When we were saying good night, Al said to me, "I couldn't have pulled it off without you." It's the best thing anyone has ever told me. I could tell he meant it, too, because he kissed my cheek and looked at me all soft. My heart may explode, just thinking about it. I can barely stand to imagine what we might do next.

I have a key to the hotel suite now, but it doesn't feel quite right to barge in. The door opens right as I'm about to knock.

Al fills the doorway, dressed in casual slacks and a polo shirt under a leather jacket. At the sight of him, my effervescence fades. My eyes drop to the rolling suitcase in his hand.

"Oh, good," he says, smiling. "You came in time. I wanted to get a chance to say good-bye."

TINA

Tariq's bad knife is all I think about.
At bedtime now I cannot sleep.
If there are monsters under the bed,
It doesn't matter anymore.
There is a monster in the room already.
On TV, some people call Tariq a bad boy.
But they have no evidence.
Evidence means proof.
Some people are looking for evidence now.
Policemen who come inside Tariq's room
Investigators who took pictures of the sidewalk
Doctors who studied Tariq before he went into the ground.
On TV, they tell the whole story.
Those policemen came into my room too.
They looked at all my toys.
I stood very still
In exactly the right place.
They did not find any evidence.

BRICK

Ty is scared shitless of what's about to happen. It's painted on his face. We all start out that way, though. Sciss scared it out of me, and now I'm tough—and all the better for it. A weak little guy like Ty, going solo without a powerhouse like Tariq to back him up? Not possible. It's in his best interest to oath in and be done with it. He can't make it in this 'hood without us. He thinks he's got it tough now, but he has no idea what's ahead of him.

To go to his dad may be fighting dirty, but I know what cards to play. That's why I'm in charge. This is one thing I can do for Tariq. I can take care of Tyrell, like Tariq always tried to. He woulda done anything for this little punk, and I feel like I owe him one.

"Thanks for the coffee," I say. I've been sitting here telling Tyrell's dad all about my plans for Tyrell, and how useful he's going to be, and what a great addition to my organization, and so on. A load of bull, but I want Ty and I want Franklin. "I'll be on my way now."

"Sure thing." Ty's father shifts in his seat. His slouch tells me he is cowed by me.

I sit straight and tall and as broad as I can and say, "Let's go, Ty. We've got some business, don't we?"

Tyrell looks to his father—for help, I imagine. For a way out. But there is no way out. And no help coming, either. This guy's a bigger weakling than his son.

"You ready?" I say. "Bring your bag. I'll drop you off at school after."

Tyrell's father lifts his head and finally returns his son's desperate glance. He clears his throat. "Well, go on, then," he says. "It's about time you start to man up. It'll be good for you."

Tyrell's features flatten. Is it anguish? Shame?

Right then, I know. We have him. He sees the whole truth now—there's no one else who will protect him. I tip my head toward the door. "Let's go." He stands up from the table and follows me. I notice he leaves his schoolbooks behind.

"That's good," I say, draping an arm around his shoulders. "You're going to be okay now," I promise him.

Ty can act as reluctant as he wants, but in the end he needs us. It's time he understood.

TYRELL

The knife in Brick's palm is the easy way. The wrong way. I know this, so why is it drawing me?

Maybe I want to turn back the clock. Maybe that's why I wake up every single day thinking about the old days.

Maybe I don't want to think about that afternoon last week and how everything could have been different. Maybe if I wasn't so scared of the street, I woulda been down there with Tariq. Maybe I woulda been shot instead of him. Maybe no one woulda been shot and everything would be normal.

Probably not, though. And if Franklin showed up, I probably would have been long gone and running.

Some kind of friend I am.

Maybe I can set it straight now. Maybe this is how I make it up to Tariq.

"We're not going to kill him," Noodle reminds me. "We're just gonna cut him. So every time he looks in the mirror, he never forgets what he did." He leans against the stoop of a building across the street and down the block from Tom Arlen's place. To hear Noodle tell it, it's the same stoop he was sitting on when Tariq was shot. Synergy, he says. Things coming full circle.

I stare over at the stone building that houses Tariq's murderer. Opposite us, I can't help but also study the larger-than-life mural portrait of Tariq that cropped up on the wall behind where he died. The debris from the vigil has been cleared away, but he isn't erased. The gray and white portrait makes sure of that. It won't last forever, of course, but nothing does.

"You can forget what they say on TV," Brick says. "Your boy T stood with us. I gave him a knife, you know. He was coming over."

"I never saw him with a knife," I insist. I'm sure I would have noticed. Wouldn't I?

"You weren't ready to see," Brick tells me. With his arm across my shoulder, God forgive me, I believe it. I can see T the way Brick wants me to, and it looks like it might have been the way he says. To just believe it lets me fill in all the blanks. There are so many blanks. I see that now.

I have to admit, here and now, that I'm probably going to do this thing. I don't take it lightly. Like Tariq always said, I'm a thinking kind of guy. I'm not the type to be rash, like Noodle, or to do it out of pride or some sense of street justice, like Brick. I do it for my own reasons, which are weird and mixed up in my mind, but it comes down to this: Tariq always stood in front of me, tried to protect me. He's gone now, and so is the wall he put up that might have saved me. It's terrible and sad, but inevitable. Jack Franklin killed more than Tariq that day. He killed me, too. Numbers don't lie, and no matter how I crunch them, I end up where Brick wants me: in a plain red T-shirt and black jeans, with a chain at my belt and a knife in my hand.

Brick still has the knife, but he's about to give it to me. He keeps putting it in front of me. I haven't taken it yet, but I'm going to. I have to.

In a minute, we're going to knock on that door, and when Arlen answers, Brick and Noodle will bust inside. They'll find Franklin, hold him down. Maybe he'll be unarmed. Unsuspecting. More likely, he'll be the sort of prick who sleeps with a gun under his pillow and he'll shoot us all dead and that will be that. We don't know, and isn't that the great and terrible thing about it? The risk and the energy and the danger and the possibility of death, even when what we're doing is a kind of death all in itself. It speeds my pulse and terrifies me, and I look at the painting of Tariq, and it's such a good likeness that I feel as if I'm really looking at him.

There are so many things I wish I could ask my best friend. So many secrets untold. So many promises we never got to live into. He was supposed to be my best man, for crying out loud, because he always believed I'd get a girl someday. He believed in me. No one else does.

Franklin took that away from me. Franklin put me here. If I cut him—I mean, *when* I cut him—it'll be because he earned it. He wronged me, and I have to stand up to that. I've never stood up to anything. I've always been afraid.

Man up, Dad says. Well, here I am. I can do it. I can stand up for Tariq.

Brick speaks into my ear, hyping me up. "Everyone has a moment. Every King. A moment where you step up or step back and then that's who you are. Forever." He leans in. "Someday, if you're lucky, I'll tell you about Tariq's moment. You think you knew every side of him? You didn't know the half."

I can't—I *won't*—believe Brick when he says that kind of thing. I knew T better than anyone. He would never . . .

My heart flutters, unexpectedly flooding me with doubt.

He would, though. T always stepped up, never back. If it was me who had died, Tariq would lead the charge for revenge, I know that much. He looked out for me. No boundaries to that devotion, at least none I ever saw. So, would he want me to do the same? It's the least I can do, isn't it?

Brick holds out the knife.

I imagine it slitting my throat. Severing my spine. Stabbing through my heart. But I move anyway.

I don't know who Tariq really was—if he was the way I see him, or the way Brick does. But I know who he would want me to be.

TINA

Tariq's knife is very heavy
But no one can see it
Backpacks are good for hiding things
People look at me walking, though
Maybe they guess
Maybe they know
Faces are not good for hiding things

TYRELL

Brick lays the knife across my palm. Heavy and sharp. Unforgiving.

I regret it already, but there's no turning back now. No way out of this. I grip the knife and trace the shape of a *K* into my palm with the back edge of its tip. Firm enough to feel, but not enough to draw blood.

"That's it," Brick urges me.

The entire focus of my being zeroes in on that metal tip. This is where I live now.

A small figure across the street catches my attention. My gaze flicks up, involuntary. My focus shatters. I recognize this tiny person.

I lower the knife. Brick follows my gaze, which lands on Tariq's sister darting down the street as fast as her little legs can carry her. Head low, backpack straps clutched in both fists.

"That's Tina," I say. "She's not supposed to be out by herself."

"I'll get her," Brick says.

"She knows me," I protest.

Brick's expression hardens. His mouth twitches, as if he's swallowing the words: *She knows me, too.* Because she does. Tariq and Brick used to take care of their sisters together—Tariq even used to try to tell me Brick wasn't so bad when you got to know him. But that was before. Right now Brick's busy being a King. This is who he really is.

"She'll be fine," Brick says. "You go on."

But Tina has become a beacon in my dark room. My focus shifts and crystallizes. The thing is, I know who Tariq was. Of course I do. Why couldn't I see it until now?

Tariq always stood in front of me. If I had been on the street that day, with bullets flying toward me, he would have stepped into their path. That's Tariq. Maybe he was a King. I don't know that piece of it. But I do know who he was. I know what he would have died for.

Tariq always stood in front of me. And he always stood in front of Tina.

Brick tells me, *Have courage.* Brick tells me, *Stand up.* Brick tells me, *Become the man Tariq will never have the chance to be.* Brick tells me, *Cut Jack Franklin—he deserves it.* He does. I could do it. Maybe I could even live with it.

If I have to use all the courage in my body today, I want to use it for Tariq. Not to avenge him, but to carry him forward.

"She's not supposed to be out," I tell Brick. "Something's wrong."

"Forget about it," he says. "You have a job to do. Let's go."

"No," I blurt, extending the knife back to him. For the first time ever, I'm standing up to Brick. I feel nine stories tall. Almost as tall as Tariq always seemed in the moments he said no on my behalf.

"Tyrell," Brick groans, "we've talked about this."

"You're the one telling me to do what Tariq would do." I drop the knife. Just drop it straight onto the street when it's clear Brick isn't going to take it back. He flinches in surprise.

"I'm sorry," I say, although I'm not the least bit sorry. I'm relieved. "I'll never be a King. Even if it means you have to kill me now, or whatever."

Brick stares at me, his expression a flashing mix of things I can't interpret. I think perhaps I'm seeing the part of him that glanced at Tina and immediately said, *I'll get her.* The gentle part underneath that brought him and Tariq together. I never saw it before in Brick, no matter what Tariq said about how they used to be friends.

I back away. Brick says nothing to try and keep me. Noodle, from his lounging place, says, "You crazy motherfucker. You wanna cross us?"

But I'm halfway across the street.

"Tina," I call. "Tina, where are you going?" I run to catch up to her, and she stops. Turns. Sighs. She appears to be looking at my shoes.

"Tina?" I think about touching her shoulder, but I'm afraid she'll pull away.

She lifts up her head. She's so tiny in front of me. "Hi, Tyrell."

TINA

Caught.

When I go outside by myself, I get in big trouble.

Where are you going? Tyrell asks me.

"It's a secret."

A secret from everyone?

I think about that.

Tyrell keeps good secrets, Tariq used to say.

Best friends are secret keepers.

Tariq knows my secrets.

Tariq is my best friend.

I'm supposed to say "was" now.

Tariq *was* my best friend.

Tariq isn't anything anymore.

Now I know his secrets, too.

Tyrell says, *I'm going to take you home now.*

But I can't go home until the hiding is done.

I open my backpack.

Tyrell looks inside and sees the bad knife.

Where did you get this?

"Tariq's room."

Tyrell looks across the street at the bad boys dressed in red.

They are loud.

They are angry.

Tariq, Tyrell whispers. Then he says a BAD WORD.

Sorry, he says.

I don't mind BAD WORDS. I'm just not supposed to say them.

"I have to hide it," I tell him. "It's a bad knife."

It's a bad knife, Tyrell agrees.

Tyrell knows Tariq's secrets now.

Maybe he knew before.

Tyrell is Tariq's best friend.

Maybe I am supposed to say "was."

Tyrell *was* Tariq's best friend.

Tyrell is still lots of things, just not that. I guess.

This is what we're gonna do. You and me together.

"What?" I want to know.

He takes the whole backpack from me, not just the bad knife.

He zips it closed and puts it on his shoulder.

Come on. I'll show you.

"Is it a secret?" I ask.

Yes, our secret.

JENNICA

The daze of solitude swirls around me like a cloud. My phone doesn't ring. Noodle doesn't even come by or try to win me back. Maybe he knows I'm not worth it. Maybe he's already moved on.

Brick sent me a text that says *come by sometime*. I'm smart enough to read between the lines. He wants me to know there's always a place for me. With the Kings. Not with Noodle, maybe, but with him. I've seen the way Brick looks at me. His message is clear: I could walk back in, and it would be better. I could stand by the side of a real man. The man in charge. Be queen.

Two weeks ago, it might have sounded good to me. There's just no appeal in that life anymore.

Pacing the aisles at the drugstore, I run into Kimberly. She looks like I do—tired. Subdued. Eyes a little red. We are in the aisle of feminine products, and she's standing there with an empty basket, unlike mine, which overflows with items I've collected but cannot buy. It just feels good to shop around and pretend. I set it down, and we look for a while at the packages of pink and purple and neon. Neither of us picks anything up.

"Thanks for being there," I tell her.

"I want a different kind of life too," she blurts. I can see it haunting her in the way her face droops. Strange, because I think someone like her could be anything.

We tip toward each other and hug, and we both start crying. She knows my struggle, and I don't know hers, but it doesn't really matter because maybe in the end of it, we'll be friends and maybe I can erase that text from Brick and someday forget that he ever even sent it. Maybe someday there'll be a guy sweet enough to walk me home and too gentle to try to kiss me right away.

"I have to go to work," Kimberly says, pulling back from me. She tugs a pocket pack of tissues out of her purse and hands me one. We blow our noses in unison. It makes us laugh.

"Oh, God," she says. "We're such a mess."

"Tell me about it."

She gives me another tissue. I dry my eyes roughly while she swipes delicately at the mascara-smear circles under her eyes. I'm not even wearing makeup. That's how pathetic I've become.

"I like doing hair," she says. "I'm not unhappy. It's just . . . what if there's more out there for me, you know?" She blows her nose again.

"I'm scared to be alone," I admit.

"You get used to it," she says. "It's actually kind of great." She nudges me. "You get to decide everything." She hesitates. Then continues. "I get off at seven. You want to come over for dinner?"

"Really?"

"Sure. Do you like reality TV?"

"Yeah, I guess." Who am I kidding? I love watching crazy people go at each other in some stupid game show.

"Cool. It's like junk food, you know? Just to take our minds off of things. I have some episodes saved."

"Okay, yeah."

Kimberly doesn't live with her parents, she tells me. She has a roommate, which seems so grown-up and cool.

"I'll just pick up some pizza on the way home, if that's okay."

"Sure." We smile at each other, and then she starts away.

Over her shoulder she calls, "What kind do you like?"

"Saus—" I start, but then I stop. It's funny, sausage and peppers is what Noodle likes. Now I get to choose. "Pepperoni and mushroom?"

"Perfect. See you later."

"Later." My stomach rumbles. For the first time in a long time, I feel myself looking forward to a meal.

TINA

Tyrell holds my hand.
We look at the tall gray gates.
No. No. NO.
It's okay, Tyrell says.
Tyrell is nice.
He lets me wrap my arms around him;
The end of his T-shirt wads up in my hands.
Skinny in the middle—
He feels almost the same as my brother did.
I close my eyes and pretend.
No. No. NO.
It's the safest place to put it, don't you think?
I think a lot of things,
But no one asks me.
"I'm scared."
It was okay to tell Tariq.
Tyrell is okay, too.
Tyrell says, *I'm scared, too.*
"Tariq wouldn't be scared."
So let's try to be brave, Tyrell says. *Like Tariq.*
Like Tariq.

VERNESHA

Leaning against the cemetery gates, I close my eyes in wonder. That baby girl of mine. No one understands her tough little heart, her courage. Rarely does she try to leave the house alone. Maybe I'm not giving her enough credit.

No. I give her credit. It's the world I don't trust. And with reason.

Mom was asleep—I could hear her snoring—and then the front door slammed. I went racing after Tina, but she is fleet. Moving with her head down, backpack clenched. Determination stamped all over her. I decided just to follow.

Thinking maybe it would show me what is going on in her head. Since she won't hardly talk about any of it.

I thought at first the cameras might stop her and startle her into returning inside, but there was no one out there. For the first time in a week, I can breathe fresh air without comment.

The vigil is done, the funeral is done, the people have all marched in protest. Now the world is moving on, and yet my own heart has barely resumed beating.

My heart, at the moment, is racing away from me, in hot-pink sneakers, looking both ways before crossing each street, like she's supposed to. The knot in my chest eases when Tyrell catches up with her. He holds her hand, and she lets him, which is a bit of a surprise. When he talks to her, she answers. I keep my distance.

When she comes out through the gates, I'll be here. We'll take the pieces that are left and carry on.

SAMMY

Tom Arlen's place is easy to find. Right down there on Peach Street. I try to steady my chest. Control my breathing. I ring the doorbell, real civilized.

A white man answers. Tom Arlen, I guess. I pull my gun, stick it under his chin. Drive him back inside the house. The door slams behind me. I lock and bolt it tight. We're both breathing hard. He doesn't fight me.

"Where is Franklin?" I whisper. "Don't call out. Just tell me where to find him."

"There's no one here," Arlen says. "I live alone."

I make him sit in a kitchen chair. Tie him to it with some twine that's loose on the counter. There's no sound elsewhere. I pull my knife, angle it along Arlen's cheek. He harbored a fugitive. That deserves a cut, at least. A flick of my wrist.

He cries out, "Stop."

"You know what you did. Last chance," I tell him. "Where is he?"

Arlen struggles against the ties binding his limbs. I'm scared now, because this wasn't part of the plan. I was coming after Franklin. I didn't really think beyond that.

Arlen doesn't speak. The TV is on, some kind of garden show. Whatever.

I walk through every room of the house. The place is clean,

smells like cigarettes and beer. The guest-room bed is rumpled. I open the closets.

There's really no point. You can just tell by the feeling: There's no one else in the house.

If Jack Franklin was ever here, he's gone.

TYRELL

I dig with the trowel Tina brought. Her small hands grab fistfuls of the grassy turf, lining them up beside the hole.

"Can we see Tariq?"

"We can't dig that deep," I tell her.

"Is he down there?" She pokes at the ground.

"Not really," I say. "Just his body. It's kind of hard to understand."

"He's gone forever?"

"Yeah. It's pretty weird, right?"

"Pretty weird." She traces the line of the letters on the headstone with a small finger.

I get the sheathed knife out of the backpack and give it to Tina. "You can do the honors." She doesn't seem to know what I mean. "Put it in the hole."

She lays it in the shallow cradle we've dug. I help her tuck in the strap; it wants to bend and move and flop out of place. We pack the dirt on top of it, pushing it down as firm and flat as we can.

"Bye-bye, bad knife."

That's for sure. "Good riddance."

"Is it time to cry now?" Tina says, which sure enough makes my eyes prick.

"Well, if you feel like it."

She shakes her head and picks at the grass. "That's what happens at home," she says. "We talk about Tariq. Then we cry."

"It's sad. It'll be sad for a long time."

Tina pats the fresh knife grave. "Was Tariq bad?"

The million-dollar question. Coming from her small, inno-cent mouth, it seems like even more than that. Like it's every-thing.

I'm nowhere near knowing what to say. I pick up her hands one by one and brush the dirt off them. "You probably knew him better than anybody. What do you think?"

Tina looks at the sky. I follow her lead and look up. Is Tariq watching us from someplace? If he is, I hope he's liking what he sees. He loved Tina. He loved me.

It's silent for so long that I'm convinced she's not going to answer. We brush off the dirt and head toward the street. From beyond the cemetery gates, her mother waves to us. I smile and wave. The sun glints off the gates like a wink. *Message received, Tariq.* We are never as alone as we think.

Tina puts one small hand in mine as we walk.

"I think Tariq was just Tariq," she says.

It makes me smile.

"That's what he always said," Tina adds.

"What?" I ask, but I already know. I can hear him saying it. All the time, he used to say it. How could I forget?

I'm just being me, bro.

Tina whispers the rest. "You just be you."

ACKNOWLEDGMENTS

Thanks to my editor, Noa, for inspiring this project and for approaching each page with an open heart (and a big red pen). Thanks to Kobi, Josanne, Laurie, Wiley, and the Fort Wayne writers group for early reads and helpful comments, and to my VCFA family for listening. Thanks to my parents for letting me sit alone on the front porch of their house to work, and to the many friends I've visited while writing this book—I'm certain that all your voices in my head and heart helped make these characters come to life. Thanks to my agent, Michelle Humphrey, for all the lists and "one more thing" notes she endures from me. Finally, a word of gratitude to the many, many families and communities who have lost loved ones in tragic circumstances in real life. I write this to honor them and to reflect on what those losses mean, not simply in the news headlines, but to each family, each community, and our world.

BONUS MATERIALS

A CONVERSATION WITH KEKLA MAGOON

HOW DID YOU COME TO WRITE *HOW IT WENT DOWN*?

I began working on this book in the spring of 2012, when the shooting death of Trayvon Martin was big in the news. My editor, Noa, and I both watched the media coverage with interest, and we found it disturbing that teen voices were being excluded from the national debate about race and gun violence. Noa expressed interest in publishing a book about these issues, I responded with my own ideas, and this novel was the result.

IS THE BOOK BASED ON A TRUE STORY?

The specific characters and events in *How It Went Down* are all completely fictional; however, the overall book has a "ripped from the headlines" quality to it, for sure. Tariq Johnson's fictional death certainly bears similarity to Trayvon Martin's real-life murder, as well as dozens of other wrongful or controversial shootings that have occurred in recent years. I was interested in pushing beyond the headlines and sound bites dominating the national media in order to confront the experiences of people closest to this type of tragedy. The conversation remains relevant and high-profile today: Since *How It Went Down* was first published in 2014, we've seen riots and violence in Ferguson, Missouri, protests and unrest in

Baltimore, Maryland, and too many additional instances of wrongful deaths of black people—whether at the hands of police officers or private citizens—to reasonably list here.

HOW DID YOU DECIDE TO TELL THE STORY FROM MANY DIFFERENT PERSPECTIVES?

Part of what is intriguing and challenging about the news coverage that follows a controversial shooting is the uncertainty. Everyone—including members of the media—takes the limited facts that are available and creates a narrative about the incident that makes sense to him or her. The controversy deepens when those narratives conflict—when people have different opinions about what really happened. It is hard to know what really did happen in many of these cases, and it is always impossible to know exactly what was going on in a person's head when he or she made the choice to pick up a gun and what led him or her to ultimately pull the trigger. It was intriguing to me to explore how not just one person but a whole community might respond to a controversial shooting that occurred in their own backyard. I thought it would be harder to explore the nuances of this type of controversy if I wrote from only one viewpoint.

HOW DID YOU CHOOSE THE CAST OF CHARACTERS?

The final, published version of *How It Went Down* contains eighteen viewpoint characters, but in the first draft there were many more voices. About thirty total. These perspectives included only a few characters whose voices recurred throughout the novel, primarily the teenagers—Tyrell, Tina, Jennica, Kimberly, Noodle, and Brick. The rest of the perspectives popped up sporadically, or even appeared only once. I first set out to incorporate as many viewpoints as possible, and to address the controversial issues of the book from many different angles. I included journalists, attorneys, gun rights and gun control advocates, and all kinds of community members briefly sharing their views. There were segments imitating TV talk show interviews, nightly news reports, newspaper clippings, and more. Some of the characters came about because I wanted to include different "types" of people, from different slices of the community. Things like: gang member wannabe, gang member's girlfriend, grandmother, young child, college-bound kid, graffiti artist, gun owner, white neighbor. I also thought about philosophical points of view that had come up in the media in response to similar real-life controversies. There's always a law professor harping on why the shooter was within his rights, a mom who doesn't believe her child could have done wrong, a witness who claims it was the victim's fault and had it coming, a rich black guy who lets himself believe it's not about race, but clothing and comportment. And so on.

YOU CUT IT DOWN FROM THIRTY CHARACTERS TO EIGHTEEN?

Yes. I ended up paring down the total number of voices and allowing them to recur more often, so that I could dig into each person's story a little more deeply. As I came up with different ideas about new angles and perspectives to write from, I worked to join these concepts in believable ways to create realistic characters. It seemed inevitable that each character's past and circumstances would color his or her perceptions to some degree—and that those preconceived notions would be either clung to, or shaken, or maybe even overturned in this moment.

WHAT WAS THE MOST CHALLENGING PART OF WORKING ON THIS BOOK?

Juggling the multiple perspectives! The writing journey involved a lot of color-coded notecards and Post-it notes. The revision process ultimately inspired me to stop trying to encompass the full range of perspectives and issues at play and focus on developing a rich cast of characters whose backgrounds and life experiences would cause their points of view to contradict in interesting ways. The streamlining served my original purpose and goal of this book—to push past the sound bites that tend to dominate the media, to get "behind the headlines" and explore what goes on in a community in the wake of such tragedy. To consider how individuals—friends, neighbors, classmates, peers—react and respond to the loss of one from their midst.

WHAT WAS THE MOST REWARDING PART OF WORKING ON THIS BOOK?

It is rewarding to think about young readers seeing a novel that reflects some of their most urgent real-life concerns. The book offers a chance for readers to consider some very serious issues—race, community, violence, death, authority, voice, perspective, truth—within the safe space of fiction. And, hopefully, it offers a way for young people to also discuss these issues through the lens of fiction, which allows for a more open and less loaded conversation than might occur while discussing the real-world issues that the novel parallels.

WHAT WOULD YOU LIKE READERS TO TAKE AWAY FROM *HOW IT WENT DOWN*?

I would like readers to come away from the book with the sense that their own perspectives are valuable and important. I want them to feel confident in saying, "Here's what I think"—about this novel, and about other things happening in their real lives. I also hope that this novel and other YA literature can be used to start conversations between teens and adults about the prevalence of these shooting incidents, and how we as a nation can begin to respond and heal from these tragedies, and hopefully learn how to prevent similar things from occurring in the future.

DISCUSSION QUESTIONS

1. Describe the neighborhood in which Tariq and his family live. How does the neighborhood play a role in Tariq's death?

2. What issues does Noodle have with Tariq? What is Noodle's reaction to Tariq's death? How does Tariq's death affect Noodle's relationship with Jennica?

3. Why is it important for Will (aka eMZee) to lead a double life? Who is Will trying to make happy? How does his tagging help him?

4. How does Vernesha, Tariq's mother, show strength in the face of Tariq's death? What does she mean when she says, "Anger would be more bearable than this sorrow" (p. 162)?

5. Why is Brick so intent on Tyrell joining the gang? What methods does Brick use to harass Tyrell?

6. Why does Jennica accept $100 to talk to the reporters? How does Noodle feel about Jennica talking to the press? What is ironic about Noodle's reaction based on what he does when Brick asks him to?

7. Why does Brian Trellis think Tariq is dead because of him? What role does Brian play in Tariq's death?

8. What misconception does Kimberly have about Reverend Sloan? How does Reverend Sloan tempt Kimberly?

9. What is Tina's reaction to Tariq's death? How does she help save his reputation? How does Tyrell help Tina free herself of some of her grief?

10. How does Will's stepfather, Steve, finally begin to understand Will's need to stay connected to Underhill?

11. Why does Tyrell visit Junior in jail? What does Tyrell learn that helps him make a decision about joining the Kings?

12. How does Jennica begin to put her life back together after she breaks up with Noodle? What role does Tariq's death play in changing her life?

KEEP READING FOR
A SNEAK PEEK OF

IT'S GOING DOWN

BY KEKLA MAGOON,
COMING IN 2019.

PEACH STREET

No one saw anything.

In the aftermath, the curb is dewy with blood. The man crouches by the girl's body. They are both now smaller than they were.

"No, no, no, no, no." He is on his knees. On his lips, a litany of sorrows.

He shoves away the iPod lying on the sidewalk. It jerks back, tied to the body by headphones. The sound of low talking blossoms into the silence.

He is supposed to press the walkie-talkie button, call again for backup.

Instead, he reaches around her puffy coat collar, presses fingers to her neck. "No, no, no, no, no."

What he sees—it's impossible. He prides himself on being a good shot. Prides himself on his instincts.

WITNESS

You don't expect it. Ever. Walking home, like usual, the last thing you expect is to witness a murder. Shootings happen around this neighborhood, of course they do, but somehow you still never expect it. You worry about it, in a ghost way. A sliver of thought in a dusty back corner of the brain. A curl of gray matter that gets woken up once in a blue moon, given an electric shock to remind it never to fade.

You expect to cross the street, avoid the hoopla, like always. There's no call to get involved. No one wants to be a witness. To put yourself out there like that, against some gangbanger you maybe went to high school with? Hells no. Not this cat.

The squad car, lights flashing, is at the other end of the block. A traffic stop, maybe. Or a domestic thing, checking up on some hipster's noise complaint over the sound of fighting next door.

It's a whole block away. You figure you have time to get around whatever's going on. There's no crime scene tape. But then suddenly you're upon them. The cop and the child. You can tell it's a child, somehow. Maybe you know the world all too well.

When you're first on scene, here's what you find:

The body looks unreal. Some punk-ass King, or whatever, rendered inert. Black coat, like a marshmallow. Strange kicks, for a gangbanger. Is pink the new red?

The sirens are blaring. Response time was slow. One cop in the area, got to the scene first.

"What happened?"

"He's dead. He's dead," the officer says. "He had a gun."

The world inverts. This is a whole different thing. You can't help it, you blurt out, "You shot him?"

The officer lunges to his feet. His weapon rises up. "Step back."

You freeze, then slowly spread your hands wide. "Whoa, man. I ain't do nothing. I ain't see nothing."

Heart pounding, skin pounding, the pulse pumps firmly in your chest, your knees, your eyes. You pray. *Keep pumping. I ain't gotta die today.*

That corner of your brain, that worried corner, is much bigger than you thought and it's wide awake now. It scolds. *See flashing lights, go down another block. No lookie-loos.* It aches. *Not my time. Not today. I ain't going down like this.* It speaks to your feet. It's your brain—it can do that. *Run. Run.*

You fight it. With another part of your brain, the common sense part. You hold fast there, knowing you might be shot down where you stand.

The sirens grow louder.

"Be cool, man," you say. "Be cool."

He's breathing hard. And you are.

More cops roll up. More guns. All on you. Just like that, a walk home becomes a mouthful of sidewalk. Becomes handcuffs. Becomes the back of a cop car and a call to some legal-aid lawyer.

On the phone you tell her, "I ain't done nothing. I ain't seen nothing. I was just walking home."

EKE

In my nightmares I see flashing lights. I see them in the glint of sun off the other cars' hoods in the rearview. I see them in the glare off the road signs and in bouncing headlights. I see a white car with a ski rack and I ease off the gas on instinct. Just in case.

I wanna fly, you know? I wanna put the pedal to the metal, knowing I can afford the cost of a ticket. It's gonna be what, fifty bucks? A hundred? I don't know. Never been pulled over. Never wanna be.

Watch the needle like a hawk instead.

Every time.

Tonight, the lights behind me are real.

My pulse pounds under every part of my skin. Blinker on. Glide to the shoulder. Lower the window then freeze, with my hands at ten and two. I already can't breathe.

Not one, but two police cars. I expect them to flank me. They don't even slow.

My car rocks in their wake. They are flying.

A prayer slides out of me, unbidden.

Relief, for myself.

Hope and despair, for the poor souls at the other end of their call.

Find a gap, ease back into traffic. Other cars rocket by me. I'm that annoying driver everybody can't wait to pass. Their slipstream is my security blanket. They'll get pulled over before me, for sure.

I'm only a few minutes' drive from the Underhill Community Center. I'll make it there before full dark.

My old car chugs its way down the exit ramp, weaves through the neighborhood. It's hard, coming down from expressway speed. Feels like I'm crawling.

Peach Street is all lit up like Christmas. Some kind of big mess.

I crawl. Watch the needle like a hawk. Use my signals.

Fifty bucks. A hundred. That's good money and all, but what's the cost of freedom?

All I know's what it's not worth: my life.